What the critics are saying...

ഌ

Sins of the Father

"THE SINS OF THE FATHER is erotica at its best. Emotional, fulfilling the promise of the sensual as it takes you on you carnal adventure rich with a wealth of erotic, tillitating images that will fire your most sensual needs." ~*The Best Reviews*

"Short and just sweet enough, SINS OF THE FATHER is a story sure to please fans of erotic romance." ~*Sensual Romance Reviews*

"It's a steamy novel of love and lust, of torment and satiation. An erotic heat to keep you warm on the coldest nights." ~*The Best Reviews*

The Hunger

"*The Hunger* is a dark, mysterious, and very sexual story. The first part is engulfed in sexually charged, frightening events. ... I hope that Jaid Black intends to continue this story in the future. *The Hunger* is a good beginning to a fascinating and highly erotic story." ~*Joyfully Reviewed*

"...readers who like horror with their romance will no doubt be quite pleased." ~*Cupid's Library Reviews*

"The Hunger is a touching story of loss, love, and hope. This story is both filled with darkness and light and although it captured me from the beginning it is definitely not for the faint of heart. Ms. Black easily draws the reader into the past and keeps you enveloped in her world of vampirism through the centuries. Though she does relinquish her hold on you at the end of the book you are left wanting and needing more. I am keeping my hopes up that Ms. Black will continue her story in the near future." ~*The Romance Studio*

"*The Hunger* takes us on a journey through both ancient and contemporary times and shows you the monsters that have existed for eons. The characters are intriguing and well thought out..." ~*Fallen Angels Review*

Politically Incorrect: Stalked

"Jaid Black's POLITICALLY INCORRECT: STALKED surprised me with how intense the storyline is for a short read." ~*Romance Junkies*

"Jiminy Crickets we have a winner! I literally held my breath through this entire story. I was both appalled and stirred by this story and its characters. I can't wait to read more from this author. Thank you for such an amazing creation." ~*Fallen Angels Review*

"**Jaid Black** has another hit on her hands. She has a way of making you feel for her characters, bringing them to life and making your heart beat faster while they experience their fear. Although it is a very short story, I highly recommend POLITICALLY INCORRECT: STALKED." ~*TwoLips Review*

JAID BLACK

NOTORIOUS

ELLORA'S CAVE
ROMANTICA PUBLISHING

An Ellora's Cave Romantica Publication

www.ellorascave.com

Notorious

ISBN 9781419956355
ALL RIGHTS RESERVED.
Notorious Copyright © 2007 Jaid Black
Sins of the Father Copyright © 2002 Jaid Black
The Hunger Copyright © 2006 Jaid Black
Politically Incorrect: Stalked Copyright © 2003 Jaid Black
Edited by Nicholas Conrad.
Photography by Kenneth P. Robb Sr. Cover model Janet M.
Robb. Cover design by Darrell King.

Trade paperback Publication May 2007

Content Advisory:

S – ENSUOUS
E – ROTIC
X – TREME

Ellora's Cave Publishing offers three levels of Romantica™ reading entertainment: S (S-ensuous), E (E-rotic), and X (X-treme).

The following material contains graphic sexual content meant for mature readers. This story has been rated E–rotic.

S-*ensuous* love scenes are explicit and leave nothing to the imagination.

E-*rotic* love scenes are explicit, leave nothing to the imagination, and are high in volume per the overall word count. E-rated titles might contain material that some readers find objectionable — in other words, almost anything goes, sexually. E-rated titles are the most graphic titles we carry in terms of both sexual language and descriptiveness in these works of literature.

X-*treme* titles differ from E-rated titles only in plot premise and storyline execution. Stories designated with the letter X tend to contain difficult or controversial subject matter not for the faint of heart.

Also by Jaid Black

ဢ

Adam & Evil

After the Storm

Before the Fire

Breeding Ground

Death Row: The Trilogy

Ellora's Cavemen: Legendary Tails IV (*anthology*)

Ellora's Cavemen: Tales from the Temple IV (*anthology*)

Enchained (*anthology*)

God of Fire

Lost in Trek

Manaconda (*anthology*)

The Hunted (*anthology*)

The Obsession

The Possession

Trek Mi Q'an Book 1: The Empress' New Clothes

Trek Mi Q'an 1.5: Seized

Trek Mi Q'an 2: No Mercy

Trek Mi Q'an 3: Enslaved

Trek Mi Q'an 4: No Escape

Trek Mi Q'an 5: No Fear

Trek Mi Q'an 5.5: Dementia

Tremors

Vanished

Warlord

About the Author

෩

USA Today bestselling author Jaid Black is the owner and founder of Ellora's Cave Publishing. Recognizing and legitimizing female sexuality as an entity unique from male sexuality is her passion. Jaid has been featured in every available media, from major newspapers like the Cleveland Plain Dealer, to various radio programs, to an appearance on the Montel Williams Show. Her books have received numerous distinctions, including a nomination for Nerve magazine's Henry Miller award for the best literary sex scene published in the English language.

Jaid welcomes comments from readers. You can find her website and email address on her author bio page at www.ellorascave.com.

Tell Us What You Think

We appreciate hearing reader opinions about our books. You can email us at Comments@EllorasCave.com.

NOTORIOUS

ഇ

SINS OF THE FATHER

బ

Chapter One

❧

"Excu-use me?" Candy Morgan stuttered. Her amber eyes widened as she regarded the man sitting across from her at the expensive mahogany oak desk. She couldn't have heard him correctly. There was no way in the hell that—

"You heard me," he murmured. His intense blue gaze bore into hers, his expression brooding. "I won't repeat myself."

Candy stared at him open-mouthed, too stunned to speak. She couldn't believe what she was hearing, couldn't believe that this man, James Douglas Mahoney III, was suggesting—no, *demanding*—the things that he was. Under any other circumstances she would have said yes. Under these circumstances her pride would only allow her to say…

"No." She shook her head, swallowing roughly as she looked at him. "I won't be used like that, JD. I can't believe you'd suggest such a thing," she added in a whisper.

His eyebrows rose, but otherwise he remained calmly stoic. His arrogant gaze wandered up and down the length of her body, all but disrobing her from the demure white silk blouse and matching white skirt she wore. So much for the casual lunch they were supposed to be having, she thought. There was nothing casual about the way he was attempting to dominate the situation.

Her teeth gritted when she considered just how much the bastard was probably enjoying her discomfort. But then, could she blame him? If the circumstances were reversed, she didn't know how she'd be treating him.

She sighed. JD Mahoney. The man who had been the focal point of more adolescent wet dreams than she could count had finally noticed her as a woman. At the age of thirty, she had waited a long, long time for this moment to be realized. But now that it was here, she morosely considered, she had to turn him down. The irony was not lost on her.

At forty, he was still as handsome—if not more handsome—than he'd been the first time she'd laid eyes on him when she'd been but thirteen. She had fallen instantly in love with the then twenty-three-year-old, but even so she'd been socially adept enough to realize that it was and would always be a one-sided attraction.

Men who looked like JD Mahoney didn't settle for women who looked like Candy Morgan.

Not even when that woman was the daughter of the wealthiest man in Atlanta, Georgia.

Candy supposed she'd aged well enough. She had an exotic, pretty enough face with amber eyes that were turned up a bit at the corners, full lips, a cheerful smile, long blonde curls, and a slight southern drawl. But she'd never been skinny, not even at her best, and she'd certainly never been tall.

If there was one thing Candy had learned growing up amongst la crème de la crème of society, it was that handsome, powerful men wanted gorgeous, tall, beanpole trophy wives. They wanted the women who ate lettuce without dressing and drank mineral water and called that a meal—not women who passionately dined on steaks and baked potatoes (loaded with butter and sour cream, of course), drank sugared sodas and enjoyed it all without a qualm. They wanted the women with limbs long enough to wrap around a tree trunk—not a woman whose legs were shorter than felled stumps.

She sighed. Delicately feminine she'd never be.

"You do what you need to do," Candy quietly said as she rose from the chair. She nervously ran her sweaty palms down the front of her designer skirt, her gaze purposely avoiding his. She would not be a whore for any man—not even for the only man she'd ever really wanted. "And I'll do what I need to do," she said with more staunchness than she felt. "I believe I should leave now."

Candy walked toward the office door, then stopped mid-stride. She turned her head, gazing at him from over her shoulder. "Regardless to what you decide to do," she said softly, "I am and have always been against what my father did to you." His stark eyes seemed to widen a bit, but she couldn't be sure. "And I'm not just saying that."

Indeed, she had been JD's most vocal champion. When her father had turned against his young protégé, dropping him like soiled goods to earn a quick buck, she had been mortified. It had taken quite a long time before she was able to forgive him and continue on as a father and daughter should. Even then, it had been a few more years before the strain between them had eased.

"Goodbye, JD," she whispered, striding toward the door. She sighed, wishing things had never come to this, wishing too that she could have lived out her fantasies of being in his bed without doing it by serving as the familial sacrifice. But in JD Mahoney's eyes, she knew, one of the Morgans had to pay for the patriarch's injustices. And since he was dead and she now owned Morgan Chemicals outright, there was only one woman who could pay for them.

She made it to the heavy double doors of the posh office and was preparing to open them when a rough palm slapped against the wood beam above her head and didn't budge. She nervously gulped, able to feel the heat radiating off of the six-foot-one-inch body that was pressed against hers from behind. He was aroused, she could tell. Whether by her as a woman or by the power he held over her—or both—she couldn't say.

"Think about what you're doing, Candy," he murmured. "Your mother and brother are relying on you to make the best decision for everyone involved."

She was torn between arousal and anger. Arousal both because his body was pressed against hers...and because it was the first time she'd ever heard him use the more familiar "Candy" as opposed to "Candace" when speaking to her. Anger because he had just presumed that her mother and brother were as greedy as her father had been. Anger won out.

"My mother," she ground out, "would never condone my allowing myself to be used like a common prostitute." Her nostrils flared. "And neither would my brother for that matter."

"I see," JD growled next to her ear. She could feel those intense, intelligent eyes of his boring into the back of her skull. Analyzing. Assessing. Calculating. That was what he did best. That was why, unlike the hundreds of other former employees her father had screwed over, James Douglas Mahoney III had managed to fight his way back to the top and now held the upper hand over her today.

"But what do *you* think is best, my dear Candy?" His free hand came to rest on her shoulder, rubbing it, caressing it. "What executive decision do you think is best for *you* to make today? Your family can lose so much. Or," he finished, "I can let bygones be bygones and your family, corrupt though it might be, will be permitted to carry on as they always have."

Candy's body stilled. "You want me to be your whore," she said quietly. "Regardless to what you might think of my family, I was raised better than that."

"You were daddy's little girl," he murmured against her ear. He pressed closer, his thick erection poking against her back. She blew out a breath. "I have no doubt that Lawrence raised you to be everything he was not."

Which made JD's revenge against the Morgan family all the sweeter to him, she thought glumly. She was sweet and innocent in his eyes — a true lady of elite breeding.

And a true sacrificial lamb in every sense of the word.

Her spine stiffened. Suddenly it all made sense. Suddenly she understood why it was that this man who had everything, this man who could possess any woman of his choosing, wanted her to play mistress to him...

Because she was nothing like her father. And because he was hoping that Lawrence Morgan, his betrayer, would somehow know from the grave that JD Mahoney had managed to turn his beloved Candace into the same person Lawrence had been while alive—a proverbial whore who would do anything for a dollar.

"What do you want me to do?" she ground out. "Have sex with you? How many times? When would it end?" She spun around on her heel, her eyes blazing into his. He stood almost a full foot taller than her own five-two so she had to push him back a bit before she could meet his gaze, but she was too angry to be intimidated by that fact. "How much of you would I be forced to stomach?" she spat out.

JD smiled, an arrogant gesture designed to further infuriate her. It worked.

"Well?" she shrieked. "Get on with your demands! I can't put my family out on the street when I have the power to stop it and you damn well know it. So tell me what the hell it is you want from me," she seethed, "and be done with it."

He chuckled, his intense blue eyes roaming over every square inch of her body. His gaze stopped at her breasts before continuing onward to her face. "I want more than sex from you, Candy," he said softly. Too softly. "I want everything."

She swallowed against the lump in her throat. "What exactly does that mean?" she asked a bit weakly. "I'm not in the mood to solve riddles."

His dark eyebrows rose, but he said nothing. He stuffed his hands in the pockets of the expensive Italian suit he wore and intently regarded her face. "Everything," he murmured, "means just that." His jaw clenched. "Sex isn't good enough, my dear. Not good enough by a long shot."

She blushed, feeling like a fool that she'd thought for even a moment that JD Mahoney wanted her in his bed. What a ridiculous notion, she conceded. She bit her lip. He could have any woman he wanted. He hardly needed to get his rocks off with ordinary Candy.

"Oh don't think you're off the hook," he growled, misinterpreting the look she'd given him as relief. "I'll be fucking you whenever and however I want. But sex is only a small part of the overall penance, *darling*."

She hesitated, worry engulfing her features once again. "What precisely do you mean?" she muttered. "You've lost me."

"I'm going to own you," he said simply, coming straight to the point. His gaze drilled into hers, his expression once again brooding. "Marry you, breed you, have total control over your body—"

Her amber eyes widened. That was the last thing she had been expecting to hear. *Marry* her? He didn't need to marry her to take over Morgan Chemicals! At this juncture, all it would take was one word to the bank and board of directors and it was all his.

"And Lawrence will know from the grave that not only have I succeeded in infiltrating his precious company, but I have also succeeded in infiltrating his goddamn bloodline."

Candy stared at him blankly, too stunned to react. JD's grand plan went beyond anything she could have ever fathomed. It went beyond it, circumnavigated it, and then crash-landed into the realm of surreality. "Are you insane?" she whispered. "You can't possibly want to marry me. Why would you sentence us both to a lifetime of—"

"Question and answer period is over," he announced arrogantly. One dark eyebrow shot up. "You have two choices, my dear. Come under my ownership and I allow your family to live in peace. Or reject the chance I am offering you to save their livelihoods and lose everything in the process. The choice is yours." His gaze flicked down to her breasts, then back up to her face. "Make it and make it quickly."

She blinked, barely able to form a coherent thought let alone make a life-altering decision. "Why do you call it ownership? Marriage isn't exactly own—"

"Mine will be."

Mine. Not *ours.* The possessive word hadn't been lost on her.

JD's calculating eyes flicked down once more, grazing over her body. "You will fuck me as often as I want and however I want it. You will cater to my every whim and fulfill my every perverted fantasy." Her body responded to his words, becoming aroused against her volition. "You will bear as many of my children as I say. You will behave as I say. You will never touch nor look at another man in a sexual way." His gaze shot up to penetrate hers. "I will own you," he muttered, "completely."

She swallowed roughly, her eyes wide.

"Give me your decision, Miss Morgan." His jaw was firm, his eyes harsh. "The clock—and my patience—is ticking."

* * * * *

Dazed was the only word that came to mind to describe how she was currently feeling. An hour after she accepted the ultimatum she'd been given, her lawyer had arrived in JD's office at Candy's behest. Robert, her family's attorney, had flown into a rage when reading the terms of the prenuptial agreement, arguing that it would never hold up in court. JD's lawyer had argued to the contrary, pointing out that a prenuptial agreement could contain *any* clause so long as both parties agreed to it in writing.

In the end, JD had firmly insisted that not a word of the document would be altered or the deal was off. Robert took her aside and privately informed her that his hands were tied and the decision was hers. Against her better judgment, Candy had signed the wretched thing, not knowing what else to do.

Not even five minutes after she'd caved in, JD had steered her into an adjoining room where a judge was waiting to make it all official. A bit *too* planned out to her way of thinking. So methodical, in fact, that she found herself wondering just how long JD Mahoney had plotted against her. She had always known him to be calculating, but this required a patience that bordered on inhuman.

Everything was happening so fast—too fast. Her opponent wasn't giving her time to think, which, she begrudgingly admitted, was probably a smart tactical move on his part.

"Do you, Candace Marie Morgan, take this man…"

Good lord, she thought, her lips working up and down in an effort to answer the question, this was insane—simply insane. As a little girl, she had often daydreamed about standing next to JD Mahoney and doing this very thing. But under the current circumstances?

This wedding ceremony felt more like a nightmare than the realization of an adolescent fantasy.

And why was this marriage taking place to begin with, she asked herself for about the fiftieth time in the last hour. No matter what angle she looked at the situation from, it made no sense. She could understand JD wanting revenge. She could not understand him wanting to marry her to obtain it.

Ownership, she recalled him saying. He wanted to own her. She supposed in some bizarre way this gave him the revenge he sought, but it still didn't explain why he'd decided matrimony was requisite to seeing it through.

"I do," JD muttered from beside her, gaining him her full, wide-eyed attention. The hand at the base of her back gently nudged her. "Say 'I do'."

She swallowed, her heart thumping like a rock in her chest. "I do," Candy breathed out. She blinked, briefly glancing at the judge before looking back to JD. "I do," she repeated.

The look of arrogance on her husband-to-be's face made her teeth gnash. She would get out of this, she told herself as she turned her attention on the judge. Somehow, some way, some day, she would find a way out of this farce — without her family getting tossed onto the streets of Atlanta in the process. She clung to that goal like a mental talisman, using it like a crutch to help her through the remainder of the ceremony.

Candy closed her eyes and took a steadying breath as the judge said the words that legally bound them together. She had never felt closer to fainting in her entire life. Fainting — or, she thought grimly as her eyes opened and her gaze clashed with a certain arrogant male's — murdering. Fainting and murdering were two very disparate actions, yet both of them seemed rather apropos to the situation.

One of JD's eyebrows inched up as he took in her expression. His smile came slowly, but fully. "There now," he said in a patronizing tone of voice, "that wasn't so bad, was it?"

The seething look she threw him didn't dent his satisfaction in the slightest, though his jaw did tighten somewhat. "Let's go," he instructed, his hand at the base of her back as he guided her from the room. "It's time for me to take my *wife* on a little honeymoon."

Candy's expression went from angry to worried in a heartbeat. She hoped he was being sarcastic and not literal. The word honeymoon implied leaving Atlanta — something she couldn't do if she hoped to work behind the scenes to get her company back. "What do you mean?" she asked hesitantly, her body stilling.

"A honeymoon," he said dryly. "That thing people go on after they get married." He patted her butt, making her yelp. "Let's go."

Chapter Two

જી

Candy hesitantly accepted JD's hand, her mouth dry as cotton when he laced his larger fingers through hers and guided her toward his private, corporate airplane. She hadn't been expecting that they'd have a real honeymoon—not by a long shot. So she'd been surprised, and more than a little worried, when her husband of an hour had informed her that they were heading for his private tropical island off the coast of Costa Rica and that they would remain there for two months.

The thought was arousing.

The thought was distressing.

There would be no one around to hear her screams if he meant to do her any harm.

Logically speaking, he didn't seem the type who got off on inflicting pain on others, but then again, who was she to say? She barely knew him. Besides, she thought morosely, she was aware of the fact that he believed her to have been in cahoots with her father. She doubted that her softly whispered words to the contrary in his office, words that had come five years too late, had made much of a difference. She sighed, wondering again what he meant to do with her.

And, damn it anyway, there was no way to fight him once they left Atlanta. She needed to be there to keep tabs on the takeover—and find ways to reverse it. Her lawyer had advised her that the situation looked hopeless, but hopeless had never stopped Candy before. She needed to find a way to get back to Atlanta—and she had to do it with the arrogant jerk's permission.

JD had actually made her compliance toward him a legal part of their marriage. She had been all but forced to sign the prenuptial agreement, swearing by penalty of her family being expelled from their familial estate that she would obey him without question in all things. Legally, she recalled through gritted teeth, she wasn't even allowed to raise her voice to him without her family being punished. Not if she wished to keep from violating the damn contract he'd insisted she sign.

Her nostrils flared. She had a feeling her family would be tossed into the streets outside of a week. Contrary to JD's beliefs, she had never been the sweet, biddable type. Sweet, biddable women couldn't effectively run billion-dollar companies. And she *had* effectively run it before the takeover. Problem being her father had made a lot of foolish business decisions before his death that had depleted a great deal of capital.

Then again, her "husband" probably knew that. She silently wondered if that was part of the lure of marrying her — getting a chance to forcibly bring a strong, independent woman to heel after slowly bleeding her cash assets dry so she could no longer fight him.

Thirty minutes later, the plane had taken off, the cocktails had been served and Candy sat in her seat across from her new husband sipping a margarita. She stared out of the window, pretending to watch the clouds pass by, too overwhelmed to make eye contact with the man who for all intents and purposes held all power over her.

Still, her intelligence hadn't deserted her. Even if she wasn't looking at him, she knew he was watching her — staring at her. The knowledge of it put her senses on alert, fraying her already wrought nerves. For years she had wanted to be the object of this man's attention. Now she was and she didn't know how to feel. Her mind abhorred his focus on her, but her damn belly was clenching in a weird way. Apparently her mind hadn't yet informed her butterfly-filled stomach that the attention she was currently the brunt of was not a positive thing.

"You have gorgeous breasts," JD murmured, gaining him her full wide-eyed attention. She hadn't expected him to be so forthwith—why, she hadn't a clue. Forthwith was in his nature. "I can see how stiff your nipples are from under your blouse." He watched as she nervously cleared her throat and glanced away. "Are you cold, aroused or both?"

Aroused, she thought, squirming a bit in her seat. "Cold," she whispered.

Candy briefly closed her eyes, steeling herself. Perverse or not, stupid or not, her body had always innately responded to the dark, forbidding man sitting across from her. It was as if her body had been created by the gods for the sole purpose of finding pleasure with James Douglas Mahoney III. No other man had gotten her aroused from mere words and simple glances. No other man but JD.

She hated to admit it, but he looked more dangerously handsome than ever today. Still wearing the same Italian black suit he'd married her in, his dark brown hair was as attractively disheveled as the tie that he'd loosened and which now lay haphazardly slung around his neck. His athletic musculature was evident even with clothing covering his body. His eyes were deep blue and intense, the laugh lines at the corners in stark contrast to the brooding expression on his face.

"Then I'll have to change that," he said softly, setting down his brandy. "I want my wife aroused for me and my cock at all times."

Candy blew out a breath, squelching the reaction to gawk at him. As taken aback as she was, arousal still overwhelmed her. This was just too much. It didn't matter to her libido that all JD wanted from her was revenge. This was still the same man she'd secretly yearned for over half of her life.

She was already turned on, she conceded to herself. If he touched her she would probably explode on contact. She firmly reminded herself that she had no business being aroused, that this man whom she had desired for so many years was the same man who had taken her life as she knew it away from her. She'd have to keep remembering that fact.

"Take off your clothes."

Her head shot up to meet his gaze. Her eyes rounded. "Wh-what?" Her heart felt as though it might thump out of her chest. He was wasting no time in upping the ante.

JD's intense blue eyes grew impossibly more so. "Take off your clothes," he repeated.

"B-But the crew —"

"Your clothes," he said softly, his authoritative look reminding her of their legal marriage agreement. "Take them off."

Candy stilled. She had never permitted a man to see what she looked like naked in the full light of day. Contemplating doing so was the most frightening thing she could imagine.

And yet, perversely, it was also the most arousing.

She really wished her libido would get with the program. JD wanted revenge — not her.

"I'm waiting," he murmured. "I want to see those stiff nipples of yours with no clothing on to impede my view."

She quickly chugged the remainder of the margarita, then set the glass down. She hesitated for a moment, but eventually stood up and prepared to undress herself. It wasn't as if she had much choice in the matter, Candy reminded herself. She would have to comply for as long as she could, or at least until she figured a way out of this mess. If such a way even existed. She might become an alcoholic first, she decided grimly.

"Would you turn around?" she asked quietly, her head bowed in embarrassment. "Please?"

"No." JD picked up his brandy and settled comfortably into his seat.

Candy glanced up, for some reason surprised by the obvious arousal in his voice. She quickly averted her gaze, immediately noting the prominent bulge in his trousers. She blew out a breath.

"I want to look at my wife, not at the back of the goddamn plane," he said thickly.

Her teeth sank into her lower lip. Painful recollections of her father telling her that she needed to lose weight, that she was too fat and unappealing, flooded her memories. *Go to the gym,* Lawrence had repeatedly told her. *You'll never snag a husband looking like a heifer out to pasture.*

"I'm not much to look at," Candy whispered. "Please...I'm not trying to go back on our deal, but I—"

"I think you have everything to look at," he interrupted, surprising her. "Now show it to me. I want to see the nipples I now own...and the rest of the body that belongs to me."

She took a calming breath, his words more arousiing than ten knowing hands intimately massaging her all at once. She didn't want to be attracted to him, given the circumstances of their marriage, but there it was. It was hard not to be attracted to a handsome man who was, whether he realized it or not, making her feel like maybe, just maybe, she wasn't as completely unappealing as she'd always thought.

Candy slowly began peeling off her clothing. She carefully avoided making eye contact but could feel his intense gaze all over her when she removed first her white silk blouse and then her lacy white bra.

His hands immediately seized her breasts, making her gasp in shock. His thumbs massaged her distended nipples. "Beautiful," he murmured, his voice thick. "Your nipples are large and long. Perfect for sucking on."

She squeezed her thighs together and blew out a breath. His mouth was so close to her nipples she could feel his breath warming them. "Th-thank you."

His tongue lashed out, surprising her, making her gasp again. He took turns with both breasts, slowly licking around the circumference of each nipple, then suctioning the tip into his mouth.

Her heart rate went over the top, her legs beginning to feel like overcooked spaghetti noodles. He curled his tongue around her left nipple and drew it into the heat of his mouth. She moaned softly when his lips latched onto it, her hands instinctively threading through his dark hair as he began to suckle it.

JD spent the next ten minutes showering her breasts with attention. He sucked on one nipple for a couple of minutes, then switched to the other one and did the same. He repeated the process over and over again, not stopping until she was breathless and clinging to him.

His dark head came up from her chest, his eyelids heavy. "Now the rest," he murmured. "Show me the exquisite cunt I now own."

Her breathing labored, her nipples achingly swollen, Candy complied. She stepped back a bit as her hands shakily reached behind her for the zipper to her white, thigh-high skirt. She glanced down at her breasts as she unzipped herself, noting how ruby-red and distended her nipples were. She could still see the faint outline of teeth marks, a sight that made her wetter still.

"Now remove your panties," JD said hoarsely as her skirt fell to the ground and pooled around her feet. "I want you wearing nothing but those high heels."

The white silk panties came off next, quickly joining the garments already lying on the ground. She heard JD suck in his breath and wasn't sure what to make of the sound. She bit into her lower lip, once again feeling ashamed and unsure of her body. Was he aroused or disgusted? She couldn't tell. She shouldn't care.

He stilled. "You shaved your pussy bald," he said thickly. "Have you always shaved it?"

She nodded, still too embarrassed to look him in the eye.

"Why?" he murmured. "Do you like how sensitive it is when you masturbate?"

Her face grew hot, giving him her answer. She looked away.

"Show me," he said, his tone commanding. "Sit down, spread your legs and show me how you like to touch yourself."

"JD—"

"Show me," he cut her off, interrupting her protest. "Your body belongs to me now, Candy. From here on out, you use it to pleasure your husband, not yourself."

She blew out a breath. The man had a way with words. Candy knew this was destined to be the shortest masturbation session of her life for she was already *this close* to coming. "Okay," she whispered.

Sitting down in her seat across from him, Candy splayed her legs wide, bringing them down to rest on the arms of the seat. She could feel his commanding eyes staring boldly at her exposed flesh, his gaze practically branding it.

"Touch yourself," he said thickly.

He unzipped his trousers and released his erection from its previous confinement. She swallowed as she briefly stared at it. His cock was long and thick, a vein running prominently down the middle from the root to the head.

"Play with your cunt for me."

Her fingers slid down and found her clit. She bit her lip as she watched him stare at her through hooded eyes. She closed her eyes and began to manipulate her clit, rubbing it in a circular fashion as her breathing grew more and more labored.

"That's right, sweetheart," he said in low tones. "Keep stroking your pussy for me. From now on you always have to ask my permission before you touch yourself. Do you understand me, Candy?"

From somewhere in the back of her fevered mind she found the wherewithal to answer yes.

"It's my cunt now," he reminded her. "And it's never to be touched without the permission of its owner."

Candy gasped as desire shot through her, knotting in her belly. She continued to rub her fingers all over her drenched clit, the swollen piece of flesh throbbing with blood, aching for release.

"Beautiful," JD murmured, his voice aroused. "Exquisite."

She came on a loud groan, blood rushing up to heat her face. Her nipples shot out, distended and swollen. Her breath came out in pants.

A knock on the cabin door made Candy yelp, bringing her back to reality quicker than a bucket of ice water to the face.

One of JD's eyebrows rose. "Don't get dressed," he ordered her when she reached for her blouse. "There's a blanket in the cabinet to your right. Use it while I see what my assistant wants."

The thought horrified her. "But I don't want him to see-"

"He won't see anything," he interrupted her. His erection was very obvious, swollen and jutting out from his trousers. "Just get the blanket." He quickly adjusted himself and zipped his fly.

Her heart racing, she moved quicker than what she thought she was capable of. Blanketed from neck to toes within seconds, she thought she saw a bemused expression cross his face before his features went blank and he called out to his assistant that it was okay to come in.

Candy blew out a breath as Tom entered the cabin and the two men began discussing business matters she cared nothing about. His assistant was trying not to look at her, she could tell, but his gaze kept repeatedly flicking to where she sat. She blushed, remembering how loudly she'd climaxed only seconds before Tom had knocked on the door. She wondered if he'd heard her and supposed that he probably had.

"That will be all for now," she heard JD mutter to his assistant. She bit her lip, watching as her husband was handed a refill of brandy. "Don't come in here again before the plane lands."

"Of course, Mr. Mahoney."

Tom walked away, his face stoic but the bulge in his pants telling another story. Good lord, he *had* heard her, Candy thought, horrified. She wanted to die of embarrassment. It was unlikely the assistant was aroused from the sight of her in a blanket—she'd seen nuns wearing less material! Besides, he couldn't have known she was naked beneath it unless he;d heard what she had been doing before he came in. The temperature in the plane was on the chilly side. Under ordinary circumstances most people would have just assumed she was cold.

JD narrowed his eyes at her. She blinked, having no clue as to why.

"Never look at another man's penis," he snapped.

Candy gritted her teeth. "Why did you let Tom come in here if I wasn't supposed to notice his, um, *reaction* to the events he'd obviously overheard!" Her gaze found his. She couldn't stop her nostrils from flaring, her anger from showing a bit. "Why did you let him in here?"

He smiled slightly. "Truthfully?"

She frowned. "Well, yes."

"I didn't realize he'd heard anything until he was in here and I saw his..." JD's jaw steeled. "I didn't like it," he growled. "I became jealous."

Her eyes widened, surprised that he felt that way at all. Surprised too that he'd admitted to it. And why, she wondered, was he jealous in the first place? She would have thought, given the circumstances, that JD would have enjoyed embarrassing her in front of someone else. The man was an enigma she wasn't likely to figure out any time soon. "Thank you for answering the question," she mumbled, looking away,.

"You're welcome."

She cleared her throat. "I'm sorry," she muttered dumbly, not sure of what else to say, "for making you jealous. May I get dressed now?"

"No."

Her head whipped around to look at him.

He settled into his seat and brought the brandy up to his lips. "As a matter of fact remove the blanket again. I was enjoying the view," he said boldly.

She rubbed her temples. "JD..."

"Yes?"

"This is a bit much all at once. Three hours ago I was still officially dating Donald Carver. A blink of an eye later I'm married to you. I think—"

"Did you love Don Carver?" His voice was soft.

No, she didn't, but that was beside the point. She and Don had only been seeing each other two weeks—hardly enough time to fall in love. "Well..."

His eyebrows shot up. "Don't make me jealous again, please."

Candy's heart felt as though it might beat out of her chest. The ice in his voice put her nerves on edge even more than they already were. He was jealous of Don?

"Take off the blanket," JD reiterated with a frown. "Now."

She shook her head slightly, feeling dazed and more confused by his confessions of jealousy than she cared to be. Taking a calming breath, she quickly discarded the blanket and shoved it back in the cabinet. She fell into her chair as soon as she was done, primly crossing her legs to shield herself as much as possible.

"Open them."

She stilled. "JD, please… I'm not used to…to…this."

"Open them," he said again, though more gently this time. His voice was thick again, his words obviously laced with arousal.

She closed her eyes briefly, then slowly opened her thighs. She could have sworn she heard him suck in his breath again, but was far too nervous to look at his face to verify the supposition.

Candy sat there for another fifteen minutes, her naked flesh on display for her husband, her high-heel-clad feet dangling from the arms of the chair. His intense blue gaze never seemed to stray from her center. He simply sat there and sipped from his brandy, his eyes memorizing a part of her she would have preferred to keep concealed. She rightly assumed he was enjoying his arousal, not at all in a hurry to do anything but look. Eventually, however, his need took over.

"Suck on me," he said. "Kneel before me and suck on my cock."

Her head shot up. Her eyes rounded as she swallowed past the lump in her throat.

Candy hesitated, feeling very unsure of herself. Glancing up at his face, she noted that his eyes were heavy-lidded. She nibbled on her bottom lip as she watched him unzip his trousers and take out his stiff penis again, his erection now as unconfined as it had been before Tom knocked on the cabin door.

The sight of his arousal gave her frantic mind one less fear—namely that he wanted her to perform on him only so he could make fun of her inability to get him hard. She mentally conceded that the thought had probably been a dumb one considering the fact that he'd been erect for most of the flight, but the thought had occurred to her nevertheless.

JD definitely wanted her. She had no idea why, but realized without a doubt that he did.

She closed her legs and stood up. Slowly coming down on her knees in front of him, she took him into her mouth without ceremony. The sound of his breath catching in the back of his throat made those unwanted butterflies flutter in her belly again.

"Very good, sweetheart," JD said hoarsely, his fingers twining through her hair. "Now spend some time getting to know him."

His words were arousing, though she couldn't say why. Because of the thick way he'd uttered them? Because of the way he talked about his erection like it was an entity separate from him? She didn't know. All she knew was that her own breathing was quickly growing labored.

She did as he requested, taking his penis in slowly, lingeringly. Candy had given head before—she was over thirty for goodness sake, but it had always been with the intent of arousing the man for intercourse. This was the first occasion she had ever taken her time, licking up and down, familiarizing herself with everything from the puffy vein that ran the length of the shaft to the tiny hole at the tip of the head.

JD cradled her face between his palms the entire time, simply watching her become familiar with his cock, his eyes narrowed and his breathing harsh. He didn't try to coerce her into going faster, so she explored him at her leisure, which he seemed to like anyway.

Candy took his shaft all the way in to the back of her throat, her nipples hardening at the sound of his hiss. Her hands came up to massage his balls, inducing his fingers to tighten their hold on her ringlets.

"I'm going to fuck your face now," he ground out. "I can't take any more toying, sweetheart."

JD rose from his seat, careful not to unlatch her lips from his swollen cock in the process. He held her by the back of the head and gently pushed into her mouth as deeply as he could go, groaning when he felt her lips against his balls.

"That's it," he grunted, his muscles tense as he began to slide his hard penis into and out of her mouth. "Take all of me."

Before she thought better of it, Candy moaned from around his cock, which she could tell only further inflamed him. He began to ride her mouth faster, his steely buttocks clenching and contracting as he fucked her face.

"Deeper," he hissed. He plunged in and out of her deeper and harder, the sound of saliva and lips meeting steel-hard flesh permeating the cabin. Candy groaned from around his penis then took over the lead. She repeatedly took him all the way to the back of her throat, faster and faster, her head bobbing back and forth as she sucked him off.

His muscles tensed and his breathing grew labored. "I'm going to give you my cum," he gritted out. His hips pistoned back and forth, meeting her every head bob. "Drink it," he panted.

She took him in all the way, gluttonously pushing the head of his cock to the back of her throat again in deep, expert movements. She moaned from around his swollen penis, enjoying the power she felt when his fingers further tightened in her hair and he began to moan uncontrollably.

"Drink it," he groaned, his entire body shuddering. "Drink it all up."

JD came on a bellow, the masculine growl reverberating throughout the airplane's cabin. Her head kept up its steady bobbing motion, her lips extracting every drop of cum he had to give. She was relentless with her sucking, keeping up the feverish pace until he was completely drained, his body spent and satiated.

He collapsed into his seat when he could no longer stand, his breathing ragged. He stared at her for a solid minute, saying nothing, his blue eyes narrowed and his chest heaving. "Suck on my balls," he finally said when his heart rate came down a bit. He cradled her face once again, pushing it into his lap. "It relaxes me."

Candy did, though it didn't have the effect he had said. Either that or they had different ideas of relaxation. Within minutes, his cock was stiff and swollen, ready again to be sucked. She gave him what he wanted, sucking him off once more before he collapsed altogether.

She stayed kneeling at his feet as he dozed, too dazed to move, so completely shell-shocked that not even her sore jaw registered as significant. Thankfully JD slept rather peacefully throughout the rest of the plane ride to the private island, because she didn't feel up to talking—or moving. Once he woke up as if afraid she had left him, but immediately fell back to sleep when he saw that she was still on her knees in front of him.

She couldn't have moved if her life depended on it, but then he didn't know that. He had no idea how tumultuous her current thoughts and feelings were.

Given the circumstances, she knew she should have hated him. She had every right to loathe him. Candy told herself over and over again that if she had any self-respect whatsoever left, she wouldn't have enjoyed doing what she had just done to him as much as she had. In fact, she wouldn't have enjoyed it at all.

She blinked, coming out of her trance-like state when it was announced that the plane was about to land. She stood up and quickly dressed herself, wanting the distance of clothing between them before he awoke.

Candy's nostrils flared as she pulled up her skirt. She consoled her injured ego with the knowledge that she hadn't been given a choice in the matter of today's events.

Anything to keep herself from having to deal with the reality that she was as attracted to JD Mahoney as badly as, for whatever reason, he was attracted to her.

Chapter Three

ဢ

JD's private oasis was even more beautiful than Candy had imagined it would be. Lush palm trees were everywhere, surrounded by gorgeous foliage in varying colors. The sound of exotic birds and beasts punctured the air as servants scurried around to see to the upkeep of the grounds.

The Mahoney estate was even grander than *Chez Ma Coeur*, the large private oasis in the Virgin Islands that had been in the Morgan dynasty for almost a century. JD's island home was palatial in size, the pink marble architecture a perfect example of Spanish influence.

Candy supposed she should have been embarrassed by her constant nudity in front of JD, or at least more so than what she was. Oddly enough, the embarrassment was no longer there. She was still, however, angry. JD had insisted that she take her clothes back off after they had disembarked, so she had been naked during the entire limo ride from the airstrip to the estate.

Her teeth gritted at the perceived insult. When she had signed on the dotted line, she'd had no idea that his revenge would extend to humiliation.

Then again, she hadn't come into contact with anyone else so she couldn't exactly label it humiliation—yet. She'd spotted a few servants when the car had first rolled onto the estate grounds, but they couldn't see her through the tinted limo windows. Still, the very idea that someone *might* see her before all was said and done had left her seething.

Five hours later, she had grown rather accustomed to her lack of attire. And to her blushes. She had even managed to quit seething…somewhat. But bathing him? Her jaw clenched. She was beginning to feel like a slave.

"Soap up my balls," JD ordered her. His gaze settled on her nipples. He grazed one with the pad of his thumb, then flicked it with his forefinger. "You'll be sucking on them quite often so use something you don't mind the taste of."

Candy's face went scorching red. "Yes, sir," she grumbled as she quickly saturated his scrotum with coconut oil and just as quickly rubbed it in.

JD closed his eyes as he reclined back in the large, ornate tub that resembled a small wading pool. He rested his head on a bathing pillow, his arms leisurely slung over his head.

Either he hadn't noticed her irritation or he was purposely ignoring it, she thought glumly. Damn it! Didn't anything get to the man? She just prayed he would tire of this "honeymoon" at some point sooner than two months. She needed to get back to Atlanta—and to finding a way to reverse the takeover.

Knee-deep in water, Candy washed JD from head to toe, scrubbing his skin as best as she could with her hands. He hadn't permitted her to use a washcloth on him, so she was forced to clean him like this, her hands that were filled up with lathered soap running up and down his muscular chest, torso and legs. She carefully avoided his erect penis, thinking some things were better off left undisturbed.

She frowned as she studied his body. If anything, she admitted begrudgingly, he had only gotten better with age. The body that had once been athletically but boyishly lean was now heavy with muscle. The face that had once been youthfully handsome was now defined, sleek and mature. She glanced away, distressed by the direction her thoughts had been going in. *He hates you, idiot. Do try to remember that…*

"Touch him," JD's hoarse voice murmured to her.

Candy glanced up. She nibbled on her lower lip, realizing at once what "him" he was talking about. Her amber gaze trailed down the length of his body, zeroing in on the large erection jutting out of the water.

"Touch him," he repeated, his intense blue eyes slowly opening to regard her. His nipples, once flat, had knotted into tiny, tight beads.

Candy blew out a breath. His arousal was inducing her own. *Surprise, surprise,* she thought grimly.

There was something else too. Something more than arousal feeding arousal. There was also the knowledge that, regardless to the circumstances of their marriage, ordinary old Candy Morgan had made the beautiful, powerful JD Mahoney as hard as a rock. Again and again.

Her hand came out slowly, inching its way down his long body. She felt his stomach muscles clench as her fingers brushed through his dark pubic hair, then down lower to cup his balls.

"The shaft," he said thickly. "Touch the shaft."

She gently squeezed his balls and released them, making him hiss. Encouraged, she wrapped her hand around his thick penis and slowly began to masturbate him. She could hear his breathing grow more and more labored as her hand glided up and down the length of him.

"Harder," he gritted out. "Faster."

She pumped his cock fast, squeezing it hard as she did so. She would have thought such a squeeze would put a man in agony, but conversely, it had just the opposite effect. He was moaning within seconds, his head falling back down to rest against the pillow, his chest heaving.

"Do you like that?" she murmured, feeling unexpectedly bold. She pumped him harder, faster. Her free hand ran over his chest, feeling the muscles beneath her palm.

"I love it," he said hoarsely. He half-heartedly batted at her hand. "Stop, sweetheart. Stop before I come."

But for some perverse reason she was enjoying this power over him. She didn't obey, deciding to pump his penis harder and faster.

"Oh Candy," he groaned, his jaw clenching. His toes curled as she kept up the relentless pumping.

He gave up, his head falling back yet again to rest on the bathing pillow. He closed his eyes and enjoyed the sensual assault, moaning and groaning as she vigorously masturbated him. She kept up the pace for a solid two minutes, watching with more awe than she wanted to feel as he climbed closer and closer toward orgasm.

His muscles tensed, telling her the moment was almost at hand. His teeth gritted, underlining that fact. But just as she knew he was about to come, his hand firmly grabbed hers, stopping her.

"I will *not*," he panted, "waste my cum. I want every drop in your body."

Par for the course, his words further aroused her, the image of him coming inside her there between them. She stood up, suddenly feeling awkward. "I—I better get you a towel," she hedged, glancing away from him, uncertain how she should feel about the undeniable attraction she felt toward her unwanted husband. "I'll, uh, be right back."

She quickly scurried from the large pool-like tub, her naked buttocks visible to him as she made her way toward the towel rack. She stood before the rack as if in a daze, her thoughts and emotions at war.

She wanted him. She didn't want him.

She loved him. She hated him.

No, she thought, her eyes briefly closing. That wasn't precisely right. She didn't hate him—he hated her.

Candy gasped when she felt his warm, wet hands cup her buttocks from behind and squeeze them. She hadn't heard him emerge from the bathing pool.

"I've always loved your ass," JD said thickly, surprising her, as he shifted his hips so she could feel his aroused penis poking at the flesh of her behind.

Her eyes rounded as he placed the tip against the opening of her anus. "I—I didn't know you'd ever noticed it before," she breathed out.

"Oh I've noticed it all right." He rotated his hips, his stiff cock again poking at the entrance to her anus. "You've got a great ass."

Her breathing grew labored. She was torn between fear of the unknown and arousal that had been induced from the knowledge that he liked this part of her body. Conflicted, she offered him no resistance when he nudged her torso down so she was bent over the towel rack.

"So round and so sweet. And so...virgin."

She swallowed roughly. That much was true. "I—I've never had a man there," she said a bit shakily, confirming his suspicions.

That only turned him on more. "Good." One of his hands snaked around her front to find her clit. "I don't like the idea of another man fucking you—anywhere." He rubbed her clit in a circular motion, massaging it as she gasped. "You're so sexy," he purred against her ear, further pressing his erection against her anus. "The sexiest woman I've ever laid eyes on."

Her eyes rounded at the compliment, then bulged when she felt the firm pressure produced by the tip of his cock slipping into her ass. "JD," she said in a frightened voice. She moaned when his fingers rubbed her clit faster, her head falling down to rest on the towel rack.

"I put coconut oil on him," he said hoarsely, his voice kept to a whisper. "Once we get the whole head in, you'll be fine, sweetheart."

He rubbed her clit harder, making her body involuntarily buck against his as she moaned. The head slipped all the way into her asshole. She tensed up on him, her body rigid.

JD rubbed her clit mercilessly, to the point where Candy could do nothing but moan loudly as he brought her quickly toward orgasm. "JD," she groaned, her body bucking up against his again. *"Oh my God."*

Candy cried out as she burst, the orgasm powerful and violent. He sank his cock into her ass at the same time she climaxed, seating himself to the hilt. She gasped again, her eyes wide with shock.

"I'm all the way in," he announced, standing still, giving her time to adjust. "You did it. You're fine," he said encouragingly.

She swallowed roughly, but nodded. He was right. Getting past the head had been the difficult part.

His hips slowly began to undulate, back and forth, ever so slowly. The fingers of one hand dug into her hip while the fingers of the other hand continued to massage her drenched, shaved pussy. She gasped, the feeling, as always, arousing in the extreme.

He picked up the pace a bit as he sank in and out of her. "Oh Christ," he howled, his voice so hoarse he sounded as though he was being tortured to death. His cock plunged in and out of her pliable flesh, able to go faster and deeper now that her body had adjusted to the size of him. "You're so tight, sweetheart. My God, you're so fucking tight…"

Candy threw her hips back at him, enjoying the way he was fucking her ass now that she could take it. It was an odd feeling, but an undeniably arousing one. Coupled with the clit massage it was driving her over the edge.

She moaned as she met his thrusts, her breasts jiggling beneath her as her husband's hand massaged her clit and his cock impaled her asshole. "I'm *coming*," she wailed, her oncoming orgasm so powerful it made her feel hysterical. *"Oh my God – JD."*

She came loudly and violently, her entire body acutely sensitive as an orgasm ripped through her belly. She screamed at the intensity of it, hysterical sounds bubbling up from her throat as he repeatedly sank into her.

He groaned as if in agony, massaging her wet pussy in fast, circular strokes while he fucked her ass harder. He pumped her for another solid minute, his moans filling the bathing chamber.

"I'm coming too," JD panted, unable to last as long as he wanted to inside such a tight hole. His hips pistoned back and forth, his body animalistically pounding into hers.

She could hear his breathing growing labored, short puffs of breath warming her ear. "Oh fuck — *Candy.*"

He came, his entire body shuddering over hers. He moaned as she continued to throw her hips back at him, her tight anus extracting every drop of cum he had to give.

"Candy," he groaned again, though weaker this time.

His fingers dug into the flesh of her hips as their undulations began to wane. "Candy," he whispered, "thank you."

Candy closed her eyes as the undulations ceased, unsure of what to say, unsure of what to feel.

James Douglas Mahoney III had just taken her up the ass, she thought in a daze. She didn't know whether to laugh, cry, scream or thank the gods that she had finally felt the object of her longtime desire sink his cock inside her body. As always where JD was concerned, her emotions were in chaos.

She'd loved him half of her life, yet she hated him for what he'd done to her family.

"You're welcome," she mumbled, for some reason wanting the intimacy between them to last. It was a moment of truce, she realized.

While they were joined like this, they were simply a man and a woman, two lovers basking in the aftermath of sex.

Instead of two enemies, each plotting to conquer the other.

JD kept uncharacteristically quiet, as if he too recognized the poignancy of the moment. Wordlessly and tenderly, he pulled out of her body and carried her back to the bath.

Candy didn't meet his gaze the entire time he bathed her. Why was he being so gentle with her, she wondered as his hands massaged soap onto her breasts. She decided not to question his motivations and to simply enjoy the moment.

Still, she wished it could always be like this, she conceded. Not necessarily sexual per se, but calm. She wished she could erase the past and make it go away for good. Would Lawrence's faithlessness haunt their lives forever?

She sighed as she resignedly accepted the fact that it just might.

Chapter Four

🔊

"I can't believe you still won't let me put on my clothes," Candy hissed. She absently frowned down at the dinner plate that had been set before her, then glanced around the room they were seated in. The dining parlor was huge and airy, the architecture Spanish.

This was the third day they'd been on the island and she still hadn't seen a stitch of clothing. Or another person, though she knew others were here. The good humor she'd begun to entertain toward her husband on their wedding night had long since dissolved, replaced with irritation. "If I had known that I was going to be treated in this fashion..."

"What would you have done?" JD murmured, his penetrating gaze meeting hers.

Her nostrils flared. She still would have married him and they both knew it. It was either this or watch in helplessness as her unskilled mother and brother were tossed out onto the streets. "I hope you're enjoying yourself—"

"Immensely."

"Because it won't last forever."

His eyebrows rose. "You don't intend on keeping your part of the bargain?" He raised a glass of Pinot Grigio to his lips. "How unsporting of you, sweetheart."

"I'm going to find a way to get Morgan Chemicals back," she gritted out. "Just you watch me."

Silence.

Candy idly wondered why she'd been at his throat all day long. Her nudity hadn't bothered her on the first or second day of their honeymoon, so why now?

She frowned, refusing to accept the possibility that she was feeling rejected by the fact that he hadn't made a move to consummate their marriage as of yet. Indeed, he hadn't touched her since the night he took her anal virginity—and now she felt foolish for having entertained such romantic notions of him after the deed had been done. Her pride was smarting at the perceived rejection.

There was also the undeniable fact that this man had stolen her company, her livelihood and her pride in one fell swoop. When he wasn't touching her or making her touch him, it was easier to concentrate on her anger.

JD set down the glass of white wine and steepled his fingertips. "You have no way of getting the company back and we both know it. Now stop being petulant and eat your fish."

She snorted and rolled her eyes. "Where there's a will there's a way. And I'm allergic to fish."

He hadn't seemed worried in the least about her threats, yet oddly enough, the fish comment got to him. "I'm sorry, sweetheart. I didn't know that. I'll order you something else."

Her hand whipped out and came to rest on his. "Please don't ring the bell," she said quietly. "I'd rather eat the fish than have someone see me naked."

She thought she saw something gentle in his eyes, but she couldn't be sure. She slowly removed her hand and glanced away.

"Did you have something to do with it?" he asked softly, throwing her off guard.

Candy blinked. Her forehead wrinkled as she looked at him. "Something to do with what?"

"With getting me fired all those years ago." His jaw tightened. "With stealing my ideas and passing them off to the board as Lawrence's."

She sighed. "JD…I feel awful about what my father did, but—"

"Just answer the question," he said evenly, "A simple yes or no will suffice."

She looked him dead in the eye. "No," she said firmly. "I didn't know you were fired until a week after it happened. It was another two months before I found out what he'd done to you." Her back straightened. "You may not believe me, because I am in fact a Morgan, but it's the truth."

Silence.

JD picked up his wineglass and sipped from it. "If you felt so badly," he asked, his voice deceptively unemotional, "then why didn't you help me?" He waved a hand. "Lawrence would have done anything you asked and everyone knew it."

"That's not true," she whispered. She cleared her throat and glanced away. She had pleaded with her father to hire JD back until her voice was raw — all to no avail. "I don't know where you got your misinformation, but my father only doted on the people he could control. I wasn't one of them. Neither were you."

"Touché."

"He left me everything in his will, that's true, but it wasn't out of love I can assure you."

"The lesser of three evils? In his eyes, I mean?"

She shrugged, though the gesture was far from nonchalant. She had wanted Lawrence to love her. It still pained her that he never had. He might have been corrupt, but he was still her father. "Something like that."

More silence.

"You may wear clothing whenever it's likely that the servants will be around, but I want you naked at all times when it's just us."

She glanced up, her eyes round. She hadn't been expecting that concession. "You believe me then?" she asked quietly.

He sighed. "I might be a goddamn fool, but yes, I believe you."

"So you're not going to punish me any longer?"

His brow furrowed. "Punish you?"

She waved a hand. "By forcing me to be nude in front of the entire world."

He looked at her quizzically. "That was never a punishment."

She snorted at that. "Then why did you do it? To make me a better person?" she asked sarcastically.

He shrugged. "I prefer you naked." His eyes hardened. "And it wasn't the entire world. It was only me. I've made certain nobody else has seen you, so quit being so dramatic."

Candy sighed, knowing he was right. Still, there had been a few close calls. Close enough, at any rate, to make her blood run cold. Yet now he was telling her there would be no more close calls either. He was almost being, well…nice.

She rubbed her temples, deciding that she wasn't likely to solve the riddle of James Douglas Mahoney III tonight. And, quite frankly, she was too exhausted to try. "Fine. May I have my clothes now?"

"No."

She threw him an exasperated look. "But you just said —"

"I said that when we are alone you will always be naked." He looked around the dining parlor for effect. "We are, in fact, alone."

Her teeth gritted. "A technicality. A servant could walk in at any time!"

"Not without my permission. They know better."

"What if there was a kitchen fire and they all came running in here?"

He rolled his eyes.

"Or what if, I don't know, a hurricane was on its way to the island and they ran in here to warn you? Or what if—"

"I think you're forgetting about Clauses Fifty-Two and Fifty-Three of our prenuptial agreement," he interrupted.

Her eyes narrowed. "What were Clauses Fifty-Two and Fifty-Three? There were so many damn clauses it's hard to keep them all straight!"

"I can provide you with a photostatic copy if you'd like."

"Arrg!"

"Clause Fifty-Two," he continued undaunted, "states that my wife shall do what I tell her *without question* at all times. Clause Fifty-Three states that my wife shall remain sweet-tempered, agreeable and biddable to me at all times." His eyebrows rose. "You've broken two clauses in two minutes. Not a good start, darling. And on our honeymoon no less. Tsk. Tsk."

Her nostrils flared. "That prenuptial agreement is ridiculous and we both know it!"

He rose from his chair and threw the napkin in his hand onto the table. "To you, perhaps, but not to me."

Candy rubbed her temples, the fight going out of her. "Where are you going?" she asked weakly. Her lips pinched together. "And if putting a question to you breaks one of your dumb Clauses I don't want to hear about it!"

"To get you something to eat," he said with exaggerated patience. "You can't eat fish, you don't want Marcel in here, so I'm going to fetch you some dinner myself."

"Oh." There wasn't much in the way of bitchy she could say to that.

True to his word, he fetched her a plate filled with fruit, assorted cheeses, bread and a hunk of chocolate cake. They spent the remainder of the meal in silence, both lost in their own thoughts.

When it was over, JD escorted her to their third floor bedroom using a back entrance so nobody would see her nude body. He drew her into his arms after closing the door behind them and kissed her passionately. His hands caressed her breasts, her ass, her vagina, her everything, as his lips devoured her mouth. By the time he raised his head and drew away from her, she was breathless and panting.

"I'll see you tomorrow," he murmured, his hand settling possessively at one breast. He rubbed the nipple with the pad of his thumb. "I'm giving you a little more time to get used to the idea of being owned by me, so I suggest you use it wisely." His eyes roamed from her face down to her shaved mons and back again. "I'm not an overly patient man."

Candy nodded, wide-eyed, a depraved sense of disappointment settling in. She watched JD leave through the bedroom's double doors, half of her glad to see him go, the other half wanting him to come back.

She sank down into the lush pillowing of the bed, a sigh escaping from her lips. Climbing between the sheets, she reached over and turned off the bedside lamp, then curled up alone in the big bed.

Why had JD married her? She asked herself the question for what felt to be the millionth time. What was it that he wanted from her? He kept talking about rigid ownership and equally rigid marriage clauses, yet for all his bluster his actual actions toward her thus far had been far gentler, almost even understanding at times. It was as if he wanted her to want him back.

Candy rolled over onto her side, telling herself it was best if she tried to forget about JD for awhile and get some sleep. Tomorrow would come soon enough. And with it hopefully some real answers.

* * * * *

JD had known that Candy would see things his way if given time. Lawrence Morgan's daughter was everything the old bastard had touted her to be and then some. She was the rock that had kept the corrupt patriarch's family together all these years. She was the brains of the company and had, in fact, managed to divert three of JD's previous attempts to take over Morgan Chemicals.

The takeover had, in the end, been inevitable. JD had been patient on each of the previous occasions that Candy had managed to thwart him. He'd known that Lawrence had all but squandered the company's assets before his death, which meant there was only so much salvaging little Candy could do.

Again, he had been right. Finally—*finally*—the sins of Lawrence Morgan had come full circle. And James Douglas Mahoney III would get the inheritance he had been promised long ago by Lawrence's lying lips.

He would get the beautiful, practical Candace Marie Morgan. He would get the woman he'd been taunted and teased with all the years he'd worked for Lawrence. He would get the same up-on-a-pedestal woman who had seemed so unattainable to a man who had heralded from a working-class background of meager means.

"She sure is a treasure," Lawrence gloated as the two men watched Candy work at her desk, unaware of their attention. "Oh sure, she's not much to look at, but she's smart as a whip and loyal to the bone."

JD's forehead wrinkled. How could he think she wasn't much to look at? She didn't resemble the anorexic mistresses Lawrence always had hanging around the office clamoring for his attention — and wallet, but he'd never seen a more exotic, lush beauty. Personally, JD preferred her voluptuous curves to the small-chested, skinny women Lawrence cheated on his wife with. "I agree," JD murmured, "that she is a treasure."

Lawrence smiled. "I'm glad you feel that way. Because I mean to give her to you, son."

His eyebrows rose. "Give her to me?"

Lawrence snorted at his confusion. "I know it's not politically correct to talk about a woman in such a way, but believe me, son, marriages of the wealthy are always arranged. Generally not put in those terms, but it amounts to the same thing. A man can't afford for his heiress to go to just anyone."

"Heiress? Won't your son be inheriting?"

"Not a dime."

Looking back, JD should have seen that as his first sign of what Lawrence was truly like. How any man could cut off his own son without a qualm was beyond his fathoming capabilities. But he had looked up to the older man, had even managed to overlook his in-your-face infidelities as a sign of weakness, because Lawrence Morgan had gone out of his way to make JD believe that he was destined to be someone. It didn't matter that his beginnings were humble, Lawrence had convinced him. Might made right. And James Douglas Mahoney III had all the fortitude and drive to reach greatness.

His eyes blazed as he watched Candy work. The unattainable daughter of Lawrence Morgan had all but been offered to him on a silver platter. To a man who had been born the son of a janitor and a waitress, it seemed too good to be true.

She looked so sweet and innocent sitting there, with her long blond curls framing her cherub's face. She resembled a lamb that had no knowledge it was about to be consumed by a lion. But right now she was only eighteen, he reminded himself, and working at Morgan Chemicals part-time while she earned her university degree. Lawrence would give her a few more years to mature and then he would ask JD to take her hand in marriage.

"I'd be honored to marry your daughter," JD said in a low tone, mesmerized by the sight of her. "Very honored…"

JD had idolized Candy all these years, he realized. He'd placed her on a level no other woman had ever been able to reach and because of it his relationships had invariably ended when the women in his life fell short by comparison.

Two years later when Lawrence had given JD the boot, it hadn't been his lost job that he'd mourned. It hadn't even been the stolen project he hadn't been credited for, a project that had raked in millions for Morgan Chemicals. It had been the loss of Candy that had made him vicious and more dangerous than he'd ever been. She had been dangled before him, then snatched away without remorse. An oasis in the desert that had been a mirage all along.

The sins of Lawrence Morgan have come full circle...

JD threw his tie down on the nightstand, preparing to go to bed—tonight and only tonight without his mirage in the desert. He knew his wife hated him right now. Knew too that despite what he'd said to Candy, he hoped things wouldn't always be strained between them.

He stood before Lawrence, stunned and vulnerable. He could scarcely believe he'd been fired, that the man he looked up to had stolen his ideas, passed them off as his own then done away with him without so much as blinking.

And Candy. Oh God...

Lawrence threw his head back and laughed. "You? Marry my daughter?" He shook his head, bemused. "Candy could never stomach an ill-bred thing like you touching her." His gloating smile dissolved into a frown. "Now get the hell out of my office before I have security throw you out."

JD stilled as the memories came crashing back. His nostrils flared. His wife might think him beneath her, but regardless she was his now. She would always be his.

He had won—*won*. He had taken over Morgan Chemicals and Candy had been given no choice but to accept him as her husband or watch her family lose everything. In truth, he had no intention of taking anything away from her family, but a sharp businessman knew when to play the right card. JD was the sharpest.

And so now Candace Marie Morgan was his. His to fuck, his to breed, his to...own. If it was the only way he could have her, he'd take it.

JD had no intention of settling for a polite, unfamiliar relationship with his wife as so many of the socially elite did. When he had told her that she belonged to him, he had meant it.

Every last word of it.

Chapter Five

ℰℴ

"Show me your cunt." His jaw tightened. "Whenever we're alone and sitting down together, I want your legs spread wide apart at all times. I shouldn't have to ask to see something that belongs to me."

The air chilled as evening settled in, inducing her skin to goose-pimple. Her nipples hardened as a cool breeze hit them, stiffening them into tight, sensitive peaks. "May I please put my clothes back on?" Candy asked. Reclining on a cabana lounger, she absently glanced down at the untouched margarita sitting before her, then toward the pool that had been built to look like an island lagoon. Surrounding the pool was a faux jungle, thickly laced with palm trees and exotic ferns. "It's getting a bit chilly."

"No," he said simply, glancing up from the computer spreadsheet he had been reading from. His eyes narrowed. "I thought I told you to spread your legs. When I look up from my work I want to see your gorgeous cunt exposed to me." He glanced back down at his paperwork.

Her nostrils flared but she spread her legs. "Is this better?" she asked icily.

JD glanced up again. He ignored the perturbed look she was giving him. "Infinitely," he murmured.

Candy sighed, giving up. She had no idea how long he planned to keep her naked and spread-eagle, but she hoped the novelty would soon wear off. Besides, she needed time away from him. How else could she plot behind his back to regain her family's empire? Then again, she thought forlornly, he was probably well aware of that fact.

Bastard.

Candy seethed for another ten minutes before she slowly began to drift off to sleep. Her mind was filled with a thousand questions and concerns even as her eyelids grew heavier and heavier, eventually closing altogether.

What did JD want from her? Why did he insist on keeping her naked and splayed out like this? Was it all about revenge, or was it possible that he actually wanted her—*needed* her?

She fell asleep in the lounger, a cool tropical breeze hitting her exposed flesh, stiffening her nipples. Her last coherent thought was that it really didn't matter what JD's motivations were. The undeniable fact was that he had done exactly what he'd said he was going to do and now he owned her.

* * * * *

"He's so handsome," Candy breathed out, a paper plate filled with a huge piece of chocolate cake clutched to her chest. She bit her lip as she watched JD Mahoney spike the volleyball a final time, thereby winning the game for his team at the Morgan Chemical company picnic. "So handsome," she whispered.

Cheers rang out from the crowd as Candy dreamily studied JD's features. His muscular, athletic body. His chiseled face and gorgeous dark hair. His…

She blushed. She was only sixteen, so she probably shouldn't be looking at him down there.

"You did it!" a feminine voice chirped as a gorgeous, thin redhead threw herself into JD's arms. "You're my hero," she cooed, her body rubbing up against his as she kissed him.

Candy closed her eyes, her heart breaking. She didn't want to see JD kiss someone else. She wasn't stupid enough to think that he didn't do those things and then some with the beautiful redhead in private, but at least if she didn't have to see it then she could still pretend…

Candy's brow wrinkled in her sleep. *I can pretend he's mine...all mine.* Her eyelids squeezed tightly, the remembered pain all too real even in slumber.

"Let's get out of here," JD murmured to his female companion. He didn't know that Candy was hiding in the shadows, eavesdropping. "I feel like making love."

Candy's eyes opened. Her heart began beating furiously. Please don't take her home, she thought. Please JD —

"I thought you'd never ask," the redhead purred. "I've been horny for you all afternoon."

"Then let's go."

Candy listened as they walked away, emerging from the shadows only when she was certain that the coast was clear. Her head bowed as pain lanced through her, jabbing her in the stomach.

She took a deep breath as she studied the paper plate in her hand. Chocolate cake was her favorite.

Sighing, Candy pitched the plate into a nearby garbage can and headed toward the gates. She didn't want to be here. She didn't feel like eating or playing games or listening to a bunch of boring people make allegedly witty conversation. She just wanted to go home.

She held her head high as she walked through the gates and toward the awaiting limo. She passed JD and his companion, who were waiting for his car to be brought around. She could feel his eyes on her as she hurried past, but pretended obliviousness to his presence as her father's chauffeur opened the limo door for her and she crawled inside.

Only when she was safely at home, after she had locked herself away from the world and prying eyes in the secrecy of her bedroom, did she allow herself to feel emotions again. She crawled between the satin sheets of her plush Cinderella canopy bed and closed her eyes, crying softly as she drifted off to sleep.

Candy awoke abruptly, sadness mingled with an urgent sensation of arousal overpowering her. Still within the clutches of sleep, her mind not fully cognizant of the fact that she had been dreaming, she gasped like a shocked sixteen-year-old when she opened her eyes and saw JD's head buried between her legs.

"JD," she panted, her back arching on the lounger. "What are you—*oh God.*"

She gasped again, her mind now alert to the fact of where she was and what was happening to her. As she lay splayed out naked on the cabana lounger, her nipples stiff and her vagina exposed, her husband lapped at her pussy, licking it feverishly and nuzzling her clit like a dog that had found a buried bone.

"JD," she moaned. She threaded her fingers through his hair, pressing his face in closer to her aroused flesh. "*Yes,*" she hissed. She became lost in sensation and emotion as the naïve sixteen-year-old girl mentally warred with the thirty-year-old mature woman.

JD's lips latched around her clit as he began to mercilessly suck on it. The sound of him slurping her flesh into his mouth rose to her ears. She moaned as her head fell back, her nipples pointing straight up into the crisp evening air. There was no more battle to be fought.

"*Harder,*" she begged. "Suck on it harder."

He readily complied, a barely detectable growl eliciting from the back of his throat as he buried his face between her legs as far as it could humanly go. He sucked harder on her clit, his fingers digging into the flesh of her thighs, holding her body steady as it began to convulse.

Candy came on a loud groan, her entire body shaking as an orgasm ripped through her. Blood rushed up to her face, heating it, and then to her nipples, elongating them. "*Oh yes,*" she moaned, her head thrashing back and forth. "*Oh God.*"

Her clit became extraordinarily sensitive, causing her to cry out when he continued to suck on it. "No—JD—please!"

He ignored her verbal plea and sucked even harder, making her scream from a combination of pleasure and pain.

Her hips bucked up from beneath him, threatening to force him to release her. His fingers firmly dug into her thighs instead, refusing to give up her cunt.

A dog with a bone, her hysterical mind kept thinking as her head continued to thrash back and forth. He looked exactly like a dog with a bone...

"*Oh. My. God.*"

Candy screamed, her back arching and her legs instinctively wrapping around JD's neck as another, stronger orgasm tore through her. She moaned as the climax pounded throughout her body, her legs trembling like leaves in a storm. "*Yes,*" she moaned, her nipples so stiff they ached. "*Yes.*"

JD gently unwrapped her legs from around his neck and repositioned them so they were splayed wide on the cushioned arms of the expensive cabana lounger. His face emerged from between her thighs, his eyes intense, as he watched Candy's panting body come down from its high.

When it was over, when she felt calmed and drugged by climax, she looked up, her eyes searching his. Candy took a deep breath, watching as his gaze flicked up from her exposed, naked mons to her face. Wordlessly, he stood up a moment later and began to shed his suit.

"Your pussy is delicious," he murmured. "As tasty as I always thought it would be."

Her eyes widened. As tasty as he'd *always thought* it would be? That almost sounded like —

Had he fantasized about her before?

"But now it's time to move onto the next phase," he growled as he unzipped his trousers. "The phase where I fuck you day and night, filling your cunt with my sperm." One arrogant eyebrow rose as he stepped out of his boxer shorts. "The phase where I get my wife pregnant."

Candy wet her lips. Would he want to get her pregnant if his sole motivation was to get back at her father? Somehow she couldn't see JD Mahoney doing that to a child, but she had to concede that she didn't yet understand him well enough to judge. She experienced a moment's hesitation, uncertain what to do. She wasn't on the Pill, so his desire could very well come true.

"Keep your legs spread wide," JD ordered as he came down on his knees to settle himself between them. "If it were possible, I'd want them that way day and night, your cunt always visible and ready to be fucked by me."

Candy blew out a breath, her arousal growing in leaps and bounds. Some women would find such guttural words a turn-off, but she wasn't one of them. JD personified masculinity with his brash ways. He was earthy and rugged — the very things that had first attracted her to him all those years back. It was getting more and more difficult to separate then from now, the sixteen-year-old's desires from the thirty-year-old's.

JD ran a possessive hand over her silky pubic area. "I've never seen a more perfect pussy," he announced in an almost absent fashion. Almost because there was nothing absent about James Douglas Mahoney III. "It belongs in a magazine." That eyebrow of his rose again. "Except I don't share."

Candy's breathing momentarily stilled. Why was he talking to her this way? Why was he praising her body? And why did he persist in trying to make her feel sexy?

JD palmed his erection, then guided it toward her opening. "I've waited a long, long time to make love to you Candy Marie," he murmured as he covered her body with his. "Too damned long."

Her amber eyes widened a bit at the revelation.

"I wanted to wait until we got to our bedroom," he said hoarsely, his cock poised at her hole, "but I can't."

Candy wet her lips, the confession giving her more courage than she wanted it to. "Then don't," she whispered, feeling emboldened. "I've fantasized about you since I was a teenage girl. Make it real."

His entire body stilled, the muscles tense. "Candy..."

"It's true," she said, blushing. She glanced away. "Please don't make me regret that I confessed it," she whispered.

He was still for a moment, as if working things out in his mind. She wanted to look at him to see his reaction, but was too embarrassed to.

A moment later she was gasping as he plunged into her. He sank into her flesh on a groan, seating his cock to the hilt. He slowly began to rock in and out of her, the sound of her vagina tightly enveloping his stiff penis heightening her arousal.

His jaw was tense, his teeth gritted. "Is this real enough for you, Candy Marie?" he asked.

"Yes," she moaned, her neck baring to him as she arched her back. "*Yes.*"

He rotated his hips and pounded into her harder—faster. She gasped, throwing her hips back at him.

"Your cunt feels so good," he whispered, his eyelids heavy.

He palmed her breasts and buried his face between them, feverishly sucking on each nipple as he slammed into her body again and again. The sound of flesh slapping against flesh competed with the sound of her nipples popping out of his mouth as he repeatedly took turns sucking on them.

Candy gasped, a groan escaping from between her lips. She reached down and palmed his buttocks, her fingers digging into the steely mounds. "So good," she murmured, her eyes closed as a tropical breeze washed over their heated bodies. "So good."

"And so *mine*," JD said possessively as his face rose from her nipples. He released her breasts and twined a long, thick lock of her blonde hair around his hand. His nostrils flaring, he rotated his hips again then slammed his cock into her, his hips surging back and forth as he pounded in and out of her.

Candy groaned with pleasure. Her head began to undulate back and forth in time to the sound of her pussy enveloping his cock again and again. "*Harder,*" she begged.

Releasing his hold on her hair, he didn't stop pumping her as he quickly came up to his knees and threw her legs over his shoulders, impaling her again without missing a beat. JD took her impossibly harder, his well-honed body able to withstand the violent pace.

Candy gasped, now able to feel every inch of his long penis buried deep inside her. She opened her eyes as he mounted her, watching as his thick cock disappeared into her wet flesh with a suctioning sound. Over and over. Again and again. He took her harder and faster and —

"*Oh my God.*" Candy screamed the words as her eyes closed and her head fell back against the cabana lounger. Her nipples stabbed up into the air and her legs shook from atop his shoulders as her body convulsed in orgasm. "*Oh JD.*"

JD growled as he fucked her, the sound of his name on her lips as she came making him go wild. His fingers dug into the flesh of her thighs as he mercilessly pounded into her, mating with her like an animal. "You're mine," he ground out, his muscles slick and corded as he buried himself in her pussy over and over, again and again. "*Mine.*"

He came down on top of her, covering her body with his larger one as her legs instinctively wrapped around his hips. His palms cupped her breasts as he surged in and out of her, relentlessly branding her with his cock as his hands possessively held onto her breasts.

His face looked pained, as if he knew he was about to come and didn't want to — as if he wanted the moment to last forever.

JD plunged into her pussy to the hilt, riding her with hard, deep strokes. His eyes closed, his muscles tense, he sank into her flesh once, twice, three times more.

"*Candy.*"

He came on a loud groan, his jaw clenched as his cum spurted deep inside her, his rigid body shuddering atop hers. He held onto her tightly, bit by bit coming down in pace until finally he'd been depleted.

Their marriage now fully consummated, neither of them moved a muscle or spoke a word for a long while. They both lay there, replete and exhausted, for what felt like hours.

Candy continued to cling to JD's body, her arms wrapped around his center. He was still holding on to her too, she noted, and he didn't seem inclined to let go.

Her eyes drifted upward. Her gaze absently lit on the silhouette of a palm tree swaying lazily in the nighttime breeze, the crescent-shaped moon behind it providing a mystical ambiance for an evening that left her wishing for things she had no business wanting.

She closed her eyes as she held her husband tightly, her thoughts on what would become of them after this night. Could JD ever forget what Lawrence had done to him? And if he couldn't, would he ever be able to view her as an entity separate from the man who had once taken everything away from him?

Candy sighed as her hands stroked JD's back. Whether they divorced tomorrow or stayed together, she hoped JD would come to see her for herself rather than as an extension of Lawrence. Otherwise, she thought sadly, they had no hope for a friendship let alone anything else.

And her father's sins would have effectively destroyed two more lives.

Chapter Six
Two weeks later

හ

"Why did he do it, do you suppose?"

Candy blinked. She glanced up from the novel she'd been reading, aware of JD's presence for the first time. Lying on a cabana lounger next to the pool, she'd been relaxing while he worked. She was wearing a cotton sundress today, one of many times she'd been clothed these past two weeks.

She squinted up at him. "Why did who do what?"

He took the seat next to hers, tugging at the knees of his trousers as he sat. "Lawrence. Why do you suppose he would turn on me like that?"

Candy sighed as she snapped the book shut. "You're looking for logic where little exists."

He shrugged, his expression remote. "Perhaps," he murmured.

"You probably frightened him," she admitted. "He saw potential in you he knew he didn't have. Lawrence was infamous for squelching the competition."

"But I wasn't competition. I was on his side."

She stared at his face, her gaze taking in his expression. It occurred to her for the first time since they'd been married that it wasn't simply anger JD had been harboring all of these years. There was also a great deal of hurt. She didn't know why the revelation surprised her, but it did. She tended to think of her husband as superhuman, not in the least bit vulnerable to anyone or anything.

"You loved him," she said softly. "Didn't you?"

JD frowned. "I'm not gay!"

"You know what I mean."

He sighed, glancing away. "I suppose I...yes," he admitted quietly. "I looked up to him, I admired him, I—"

"Loved him."

He smiled a bit sadly. "Like a father," he murmured.

Candy's eyes flicked over his face. "I know how you feel," she whispered. She swallowed against the lump of emotion in her throat, a feeling of connection and camaraderie with her husband forged in that moment. "I loved him too. He didn't love me back."

JD stilled. "I'm sorry he made you feel that way," he said in low tones, his intense blue eyes finding hers, "but I know that Lawrence did love you."

She blew out a breath, looking away.

"In as much as Lawrence Morgan could love another person, he did love you, Candy."

She stared unblinking at the pool. "Why are you saying this to me?" she asked, her voice catching in her throat. "I should be the one trying to make amends on my father's behalf to you, not you to me."

She didn't particularly want JD to show her so much caring. It made it more difficult to keep the walls around her heart intact. For the past two weeks he'd been getting under her skin and she didn't particularly want him there.

What if she fell in love with him? Or worse yet, what if she fell in love with him and then he left her? At least if he had their marriage dissolved at this juncture she could still forge onward.

She hoped.

"Because you needed to hear it. And because it's the truth." He stood up, staring at her, briefly hesitating before turning to leave. "I need to get some work done. I'll see you tonight at dinner."

Candy watched him walk away, her stomach muscles clenching. He kept trying to reach out to her, to forge a bond where she didn't want one ever since the evening they'd consummated their marriage. He was getting to her. He was getting to her so badly that it frightened her. Yet in that moment she felt guilty about the fact that she'd attempted to rebuff all of his overtures toward her these past two weeks simply because she was scared.

He was trying to be her friend. He didn't have many friends.

"JD," she called out.

He stilled, but didn't turn around to face her.

"Thank you," she said softly.

He was quiet for a long moment. "You're welcome," he murmured.

* * * * *

"Hi."

JD glanced up, his expression a bit startled. Candy supposed she couldn't blame him for his surprise. In the two plus weeks she'd been on the island, this was the first time she had ever actively sought out his company.

"Uh…hi." JD closed the ledger he had been writing notes in and motioned for her to have a seat on the other side of his desk. "What can I help you with?"

Candy smiled. The man didn't know how to be anything less than formal and businesslike. Running a company was all he knew. Being in charge was a way of life. She realized he didn't have many friends, but found herself wondering for the first time if he had any at all.

From what she could gather of his lifestyle, he worked himself to the bone, which would leave little time for social relationships. For executives with easygoing personalities who liked maintaining various superficial acquaintances, such a situation wouldn't prevent them from having a ton of social contacts. But for a man like JD who rarely smiled, was overly serious and didn't trust others to boot...

"I was thinking," Candy said as she took the seat across from his desk, "that it might be fun if we went to see a movie or something. Maybe go out to eat." She glanced around his island office, having never been inside it before. It looked about like she'd expected—mostly bare with a few personal items neatly scattered around. "What do you think?"

Those intense eyes of his bore into hers. "You, uh...you want to go out to eat?" He cleared his throat. "With me?"

"Well yeah." She grinned. "Being my husband and all, you seemed the logical choice."

She could have sworn she saw a bit of red stain his cheeks. An observation that made her heart thump pleasurably in her chest.

He blew out a breath. "All right. What movie would you like to see? Where would you like to eat?"

She stretched her hands. "Is there any place on the island to go?"

He frowned as he thought the question over. "No," he said quietly. "No, there isn't. I'm sorry." He looked genuinely disappointed.

Candy straightened in the chair, still smiling. "That's all right. Why don't we do something else? Maybe we can just skip the movie, take a boat ride to the mainland and tool around for the day. If you're not too busy, of course."

JD stilled. His gaze flicked over her face, studying it. "I'm not too busy for you," he murmured.

Her heart began to palpitate, dramatically beating in her breast. "Good," she squeaked. She cleared her throat. "Good," she said a bit louder. She stood up, nervously ran her palms down the front of her cotton dress and smiled. "I've never been to Costa Rica. This should be fun."

He was quiet for a long moment, leaving Candy decidedly nervous. She wondered for one horrified moment if she'd read him wrong and that he didn't want to take time away from his work to spend with her instead. Her pulse began to drop, her smile fading.

"I agree," JD said as he stood. His smile came slowly, but when it came it damn near took her breath away with its genuineness and masculine beauty. "I know of a terrific little Spanish restaurant I think you'll enjoy."

Candy took a deep breath and exhaled as he rounded the desk and joined her. She grinned up to him as he threaded his larger fingers through her comparatively smaller ones. "That sounds wonderful."

JD's gaze clashed with hers. She blinked, not recognizing the expression on his face. On any other man she would have called it happiness, perhaps even gratefulness, but on him she just couldn't tell.

He slowly lifted one of her hands, the one that was threaded through his, and raised it to his lips. Her heart began drumming like mad again as he gently kissed it.

"Thank you," JD said softly, his eyes tracking her expression.

Candy swallowed roughly, a shiver running up and down her spine. "You're welcome," she breathed out.

Chapter Seven
One week later

ဢ

Candy sank down on her husband's cock, impaling herself in one smooth thrust. She sighed breathily, enjoying the feeling of having her body stuffed full of him.

"Candy," JD said groggily. It was the middle of the night. And the very first time she had ever initiated sex between them. "What are you — oh sweetheart, that feels so good."

She gently smiled as she slowly rode up and down the length of his rock-hard shaft. Her hands came down to massage his chest, her fingers running over his tight male nipples as she made love to him.

JD sucked in his breath. His teeth gritted. "Oh baby — goddamn I love your pussy."

And she loved his cock.

And him.

That revelation had woken her up tonight from a peaceful sleep. She loved him. She had always loved him. It didn't matter what had happened in the past. Somehow she would find a way to make things right.

He had become more than a man to her these past few weeks — he had become her best friend too. What was more, she knew she was his best friend as well. She realized that connection meant more to him than anything else. He could marry anyone. He could breed anyone. But he couldn't reach out, wanting to be this close with just anyone.

Over the past three weeks, JD had come to mean more to her than she'd ever thought possible. In stark contrast to the first few days of their married life, her husband had revealed the gentle, kind side of himself that he apparently reserved for her and her alone.

She'd paid a great deal of attention over the years to how he interacted with others. He was autocratic, domineering, unwilling to compromise—but with her he was somehow different. During the past three weeks she couldn't recall one personal decision he had made without consulting with her first. From what they would eat for breakfast to what stocks she thought he should invest in, he valued her opinion.

Where JD was loud and a bit harsh with others, he was gentle and soft-spoken with her. He didn't seem too interested in the feelings of very many people, but conversely, her feelings seemed to matter to him more than his own.

She liked that—needed it, even. It made her feel special. It made her feel desirable.

It made her feel loved.

"I missed you," she whispered, throwing a lock of blonde ringlets over her shoulder. She smiled down to him as she continued to slowly ride him. "I didn't want to wait until morning."

JD's gaze clashed with hers. He didn't smile, but she saw something gentle in his eyes. "Never apologize," he murmured, his hands finding her hips. "I missed you too, sweetheart."

Their gazes locked and held as they made love. He looked almost vulnerable to her, if such a thing were possible where James Douglas Mahoney III was concerned. Perhaps she was being overly romantic, perhaps what she saw in those murky blue eyes was nothing but fatigue and arousal, but she liked to think that there was more to it than that.

"Kiss me," she whispered. "I need to be closer to you."

Again, that gentling in his eyes. "Come here," he murmured, one strong hand reaching up to bend her head down to meet his. He thrust his tongue inside, meeting hers.

They kissed long and leisurely, the same as they made love. They took their time exploring each other's bodies, neither of them in any rush to stop in the name of sleep.

Candy raised her head and smiled down to him as she ran her fingers through his dark hair. She continued to ride him slowly, her pussy enveloping and re-enveloping his cock over and over, again and again.

This is how it should be, she thought. This is how she wanted it to be. She'd never felt closer to another human being in her entire life.

Candy sighed contentedly as they made love, wishing that this night never had to end.

* * * * *

Candy rustled through the paperwork on the desk in JD's private study, careful to keep quiet so she wouldn't be caught. He had been asleep for over two hours, she reminded herself, and soundly at that. All would be well.

A part of her felt guilty for going behind his back and looking through his things like this, but the other part of her needed answers. She wanted to know what had become of her family since JD hadn't been inclined to discuss them with her. Her thoughts turned to the conversation they'd had last night in their bedroom following dinner.

"There's plenty of time for that," he hedged. "I don't wish to discuss the Morgan family tonight."

"But JD – "

"Please," he said quietly, his mesmerizing blue eyes snagging hers. "Not tonight," he murmured. "I'd rather concentrate on getting my heir or heiress in your belly."

"At some point we have to talk," she said, glancing away.

"We talk plenty, don't we? About lots of things." He walked across the room and stood beside her, his hand coming up to gently knead her shoulder.

She bit her lip. "I meant about my family."

He sighed. "I know what you meant. But please, Candy, not tonight..."

He had made love to her then, which hadn't come as any surprise. In fact, JD had taken her so many times over the past three plus weeks that she would be surprised if it turned out she *wasn't* pregnant. On the stairs, in the dining parlor, by the pool, in his office, in their bed, missionary, doggy, woman on top, spooning—they'd done it in every way imaginable and in ways she hadn't previously thought possible.

Her husband seemed almost obsessed with her, Candy thought as she rifled through his desk drawers. Like he had plotted for years to have her all to himself and was making the most of the situation now that she was ensnared.

That was probably true. But was his motivation revenge...or something more?

One part of her believed that JD had fallen for her, but the other part kept feeding her doubts. Either way, she needed to know. By finding out what had become of her family when he'd planned their shotgun wedding, she was pretty certain she would have her answers. After all, if you loved a woman and wanted to keep her happy, you could hardly throw her family out on the street.

Candy cursed under her breath when she came to a drawer that was locked. *Stay focused, Candy. You need to find out what happened.* She impatiently glanced around for a key, sighing when she couldn't find one. *He's no fool,* she thought. *All the answers have to be in this drawer. Why else would he have locked it?*

Her forehead wrinkled as she considered the puzzle before her in a logical fashion. JD wouldn't leave the key in plain sight, she knew, but as busy a man as he was, she doubted if he kept it far from the desk. He'd want it easily accessible...

She glanced around, her eyes darting back and forth. A photograph of his deceased parents on one wall, an original Picasso on another, a clay urn that looked Egyptian in origin —

Her gaze flew back to the photo of his deceased parents. She stilled, chewing that over. JD wouldn't be that sentimental...would he?

Her eyes unblinking, Candy slowly walked toward the far left wall of the office, coming to a halt before the aged photograph. They looked happy in the scene, she thought. Dressed in wedding clothing, grinning at each other as if they'd never seen a happier day, the bride and groom resembled two lovesick puppies as each lifted a piece of wedding cake to the other's mouth.

Candy blinked, remembering the key. And the fact that time was of the essence.

She shook off the reverie and slowly lifted her hands to the portrait. Twisting her robe-clad body so she could easily glance behind it, she somehow wasn't surprised when she found a small key taped to the back of it. *So he is that sentimental.*

Quickly and carefully removing the key, she settled the portrait against the wall and scurried back over to the desk. *Come on, come on. He could wake up at any time.*

She sank the key into the socket. A perfect fit.

Breathing deeply, Candy opened the desk drawer, hoping to find some sort of paperwork that would explain what had become of her family. There were no phones on the island. Only the single cell phone JD carried in his pocket like an appendage.

Her hand stilled as the drawer opened. Her forehead wrinkled. There was nothing inside the drawer, she thought, perplexed. Nothing but a...

"Photo album?" she murmured aloud.

Confused and more than a little curious, Candy reached for the expensive leather album and plucked it up from its previous confinement. The leather looked worn, as if her husband had spent many hours looking through the photographs inside.

Her heart wrenched as she wondered to herself just whose pictures would be inside. The redhead, perhaps? Or some other beautiful, statuesque woman he'd had to give up in order to see his revenge against the Morgans through?

Her heart beating madly, Candy laid the leather-jacketed book down on the desk and thrust it open. Feeling sick at her stomach at the thought of who might be inside, she told herself she didn't care, but knew that she did. Her hand stilled as she came to the first photograph.

"It's me," she whispered. She thumbed through the album, quickly scanning the contents of every page. "These pictures are all of me."

Stunned, and more confused than ever before, Candy went back to the beginning and took her time studying the photographs. There she was at eighteen, shyly smiling up at her prom date. At nineteen when she'd been promoted to a VP's assistant at Morgan Chemicals. At twenty when Mother had thrown a ball in her name. At twenty-one when she'd graduated from Harvard. At twenty-two when she'd been promoted to the vice-president of marketing...

"My God," she cried out, "what is going on?"

"I should have hid that better," JD muttered from across the room, inducing her breathing to still. She glanced up, noting that he had put on his trousers but nothing else before he'd come to find her.

"JD," she murmured, her eyes unblinking. "What is this?"

One eyebrow came up sardonically. "You don't recognize yourself?" He sighed as he absently scratched his chin and looked away. "It's you, Candy," he said softly. "All of the photos are of you."

She could see that. But she was still too shocked to speak. No man had thought enough of her before to so much as keep her picture in his wallet, yet JD had built a leather-encased shrine to her.

Candy simply watched him, too stunned to speak, waiting for him to reveal more.

"Lawrence promised you to me," he murmured, standing up straight from his previous slouch against the wall. "For years, I was told that you and I would be married one day."

Her eyes widened.

JD shoved his hands in the pockets of his trousers. "But Lawrence set me up and fired me for things I never did. And then you were gone." He sighed, his blue gaze at last meeting hers. "I spent years believing you would be mine one day, Candy Marie. The job, the money—none of it meant a damn thing. But I couldn't accept losing you too. Not when I'd worked so hard all of those years to make you proud of me."

Goosebumps traveled down her spine. "Proud of you?" she whispered, her heartbeat quickening. "Why on earth would you think I wouldn't be proud of you as is?"

He shrugged, but she could tell the subject was a painful reminder of something. Perhaps his past. A past she knew almost nothing of.

"Because I was a nobody," he said. "I was a nobody in love with a somebody. Aspiring to marry you was like a coal miner aspiring to marry royalty."

She felt tears gathering in the backs of her eyes. "You loved me?"

His intense gaze bore into hers. "Always," he whispered.

She blinked, her eyelashes batting back the tears that kept threatening to fall. She closed the album and ran a hand over the leather exterior, then carefully placed it back in the drawer. In a daze, she looked back up to her husband. "I don't know what to say." She took a deep breath. "It certainly puts a new perspective on things."

JD stared at her for what felt like forever before he spoke again. "Yes, it does."

She nibbled on her lower lip. There was something different about him now. As if he'd been hoping she'd say or do something she hadn't done.

Like admit that she had always loved him too?

Candy wasn't given any time to sort out her dazed emotions. The next thing she knew, JD was walking into the office and rifling through his desk drawers.

"Here," he said, handing her a piece of paper. She glanced down, noting that it was the very paper she needed to hold on to Morgan Chemicals. "I now realize that you didn't have anything to do with it. I never should have tried to make you pay for what your father did. He took you away from me. But it's taken me all of this time to realize that I never really had you."

Her eyes widened. In surprise, in alarm of what she feared he was about to say—she didn't know.

"Go back to Atlanta," he murmured.

"JD—"

"Please," he said softly, his eyes closing for a brief moment. He ran a weary hand over his stubbly jaw. "I thought I could settle for taking you by force, but I guess I'm not as ruthless as I hoped I was."

He walked away from her then, his face carefully stoic. He stopped at the doors before walking over the threshold, long enough to look back at her with those lost, haunted eyes of his. Now she understood why they were always so intense when she was near him. He had done all of this just so he could have *her*. It had never been about revenge. "I love you, Candy Marie. Now. Then. Always."

And then he was gone.

Candy's hand flew up to cover her mouth. Numb, she sank down into the leather chair behind the desk and stared at nothing for the better part of an hour. She felt like she was dreaming. She felt lost in the surreal haze that had engulfed her.

James Douglas Mahoney III loved *her*? He had always loved *her*? Ordinary, unglamorous Candace Marie Morgan?

She swallowed roughly. As if some invisible dam broke inside her, she gasped and let the tears fall freely.

She had always loved him too. Now. Then. Always. Just as he'd said to her. She should have spoken up. She should have told him how she felt...

Snapping out of her previous stupor, Candy bolted up from the leather chair and raced from the office. It couldn't be too late, she told herself. It just couldn't be.

The robe she wore dangled open as she raced to find JD. Heedless of her exposed body, she flew up the stairs, not stopping until she reached their bedroom. By the time she thrust open the double doors, her breathing was labored and perspiration dotted her forehead.

He was gone, she thought, her heart wrenching as she looked around the room that had once been filled with her husband's personal items. He was already gone.

"Oh no," she whispered, sinking down onto the bed. "Oh JD."

Chapter Eight
Three days later

രൂ

JD sighed as he glanced around the empty medieval-looking estate he'd had built over a year ago. He was the only person of money and prestige in Atlanta who didn't own a home with either a Victorian design or one with an antebellum influence. He had gone for the Baroque look because Lawrence had once mentioned that it was Candy's favorite.

He poured himself a brandy and plopped down on a chair before the large, Old World-style fireplace. He had been foolish to let her go, he decided. Perhaps he could have lived with taking her by force if it was the only way he could have her.

It certainly beat the hell out of being without her.

Lost in his thoughts, he absently glanced toward the oversized chair on the far side of the library. He sipped from his brandy as he looked back to the fireplace—then did a double take.

Candy.

She was here. Naked, sitting on the oversized chair, her legs splayed wide, dangling from either arm.

JD quickly set down his brandy before he spilled it.

"That was pretty unsporting of you to go back on our agreement," Candy said as her right hand lazily stroked that delicious, bald cunt of hers. "Don't one of those eight thousand clauses of yours cover what happens to the recalcitrant husband when he walks out on his wife?"

He sat there for a long moment, simply staring at her. "No," he murmured at last, rising up from his chair. His penis was so swollen it ached. "They don't."

Candy raised one blonde eyebrow. "Then I want you to sign a new agreement tomorrow. Because if you walk out on me again—"

"I never walked out. I thought you didn't want me."

"Because if you walk out on me again then I reserve the right to—well, I don't know what right I want precisely. I'll have to figure that out." That gorgeous eyebrow of hers shot up again. "We can make that Clause Eight Zillion and Nine."

JD held back a smile. "Why are you here?" he whispered.

She sighed as if she was the sole martyr for the entire female race and he was the idiot male representing the opposition. Much to his surprise, she pulled a photostatic copy of their marriage agreement from behind her and held it up. He blinked.

"According to Clause Seventy-Six, I, the undersigned, am supposed to offer my body as a sperm receptacle to my husband twice daily, every day, for as long as we both shall live."

JD winced at the callous wording of the document. He glanced away, clearing his throat.

"I haven't offered myself as a sperm receptacle in three days. That means I owe you six orgasms. I'm nothing like Lawrence. I always keep my part of a bargain, you see."

His intense gaze found hers. "Is that what this is?" he murmured. "Keeping your end of a deal?"

Her eyes gentled. "Of course not," she whispered, her demeanor growing serious. She rose up from the oversized chair and stood before him.

"Then what is it?"

She smiled. "I love you, JD," she told him. "I've loved you since I was a little girl and I'll go on loving you for the rest of my life."

His eyes searched her face as if looking for the truth.

"If you would have given me time to recover from the greatest shock of my life before dashing off to Atlanta like the dramatic, ill-fated heroine of a gothic novel, I would have said those words three days ago."

He grinned. Their gazes clashed and locked.

"It's been the worst three days of my life," he admitted.

"Mine too." She smirked. "But let's put the past behind us. All of it," she added meaningfully. She cocked her head. "Okay?"

For an answer, he kissed her. One minute she was on her feet and the next minute she was swept up into his arms, her tongue seeking his, as he carried her over to the rug before the fireplace. He came down on his knees and set her before him, growling into her mouth as her hands feverishly plucked at his clothing.

"I want you so much," she whispered as she tore her lips away from his. Her voice sounded breathless, her lips looked well-kissed. "I used to lie in bed at night when I was a girl and fantasize about being in your arms, in your bed."

He both hated and loved what the confession did to his heart. Hated it because men weren't supposed to be affected by words like that to the point of grinning like idiots, and yet he was. Loved it because it meant that this moment was real—and that Candace Marie Morgan was finally all his.

Without force.

JD nudged his wife down to the floor, thrusting her legs apart as he came down on top of her. Desperate to be inside her, he impaled her with his swollen cock, seating himself to the hilt. "You don't want to know," he panted, "how many of my masturbation fantasies you've starred in."

She grinned back, apparently loving that confession. He rotated his hips and slammed into her again, causing her expression to go serious as she hissed.

Candy thrust her breasts toward him. "I love it when you suck on my nipples while we fuck," she breathily admitted. "Could you do that again?"

Could he? It was damn near all he'd thought about these past three days and nights.

JD lowered his face down to her breasts with a growl, his tongue wrapping around one of her erect nipples. He vigorously sucked on it as he plunged into her flesh, his hips rocking back and forth as he buried his cock inside her over and over, again and again.

Just as he'd always wanted it to be. Just as it now was.

The sins of Lawrence Morgan have come full circle...

As he made love to his wife, it occurred to JD that he had accomplished something far more meaningful than infiltrating Lawrence's precious company, something far more powerful than infiltrating the bastard's precious bloodline.

He had managed to find happiness with Lawrence's daughter. He had infiltrated Candy's heart and she his. Everything was finally as it should be.

JD smiled down at his wife as he made love to her, all thoughts of the past firmly relegated to the cobwebs of his memories.

Epilogue
Five years later

ജ

"He's so handsome," Candy breathed, a paper plate filled with a huge piece of chocolate cake clutched to her chest. She bit her lip she watched JD Mahoney spike the volleyball a final time, thereby winning the game for his team at the Morgan-Mahoney Chemical company picnic. "So handsome," she whispered.

Cheers rang up from the crowd as Candy dreamily studied JD's features. His muscular, athletic body. His chiseled face and gorgeous dark hair. His…

She smiled. They'd made love less than three hours ago. She shouldn't be thinking about that already.

"You did it!" a feminine voice chirped as a gorgeous, petite brunette threw herself into JD's arms. "You're my hero," she said excitedly, her tiny, perfect hands settling on his cheeks.

JD grinned. "Your hero, huh?" He tickled her until she squealed. "Give daddy a kiss, munchkin."

Candy closed her eyes, her heart soaring. She still couldn't believe how happy she was. After all of these years as his wife, she still got weak-kneed at the very sight of him. Life had turned out better than she'd ever dreamed possible.

"Candy, honey," JD called from across the field. "Where are you?"

She opened her eyes and smiled. "Right here," she piped up, waddling out of the shadows to meet up with him and their daughter. Her pregnant stomach was so huge she felt like she was about to pop.

His intense gaze possessively flicked over her swollen belly, then up to her breasts and face. "You ready to go home, babe?"

"Definitely."

JD's face scrunched up as he lassoed one muscular arm around her. "Something wrong, sweetheart?"

Candy smiled up at him. She shook her head, then laid it against his shoulder as the three of them walked toward the awaiting limo. "Not at all," she whispered. "Everything is very right."

THE HUNGER

એ

The Legend
Zagros foothills of Mesopotamia
7012 B.C.

Clamping a hand over her mouth to stave off her own screams, Maltheria fell to her knees and hysterically prayed to the gods that they might save the very girl-child being sacrificed to them. "Vampiri," she whimpered from the stone step she fell upon. "Mine own."

The ziggurat temple's high priest made a dismissive gesture with his hand, indicating to his minions that the altar had been prepared and it was time to stretch the ten-year-old girl's body out upon it. The child began to cry, her eyes wild with fear.

A dark formation of clouds coalesced in the daylight sky, casting dark shadows as far as the eye could see. When all was readied, the high priest held his arms up to the crowd assembled at the stone steps below and boomed out the ritualistic words so familiar to them all.

"I offer unto you the life's blood of this child in exchange for the life's blood of the crops. May the gods be well pleased with this unworthy sacrifice and deliver unto us the rains."

Maltheria's eyes widened in horror at the sound of her daughter's tortured scream. A wooden stake was driven through Vampiri's heart, the blood of her innocent body gushing obscenely from the hideous puncture wound and dripping into a clay urn positioned below the slab of stone she had been strapped to. A horrific gurgling sound bubbled up from her daughter's chest as her life's blood poured from the hole, dripping a pristine red into the ritual urn.

"*Vampiri*," Maltheria sobbed as her eldest son, Malleus, clutched her hand. Hysterical with grief, she shot to her feet and tried to break from her son's grasp that she might do — she didn't know what she might do, only that her daughter needed her.

"Mother, do not!" Malleus pleaded in a fervent whisper. "They will slay you too. This you know."

But Maltheria was beyond reason, beyond sanity. With the berserk instincts of an animal protecting her young, she snatched her small hand from her son's larger one with a brute strength never before known to her and raced up the stone steps of the ziggurat. "Vampiri," she wailed, tears tracking her cheeks, "Mama comes, daughter!"

A stinging blow to her face dealt by the high priest caused Maltheria to lose her footing and plunge directly toward her daughter's lifeless body. Weeping, she fell on Vampiri just below the heart, her eye nearly impaled by the other end of the jutting pike.

The dark clouds overhead began to rumble, growing black as sackcloth. The moon and the sun merged as one, forming a solitary crimson stain in the black skies.

"Fool woman!" the high priest spat, hoisting Maltheria up from her daughter's body by a jerk to her raven-black hair. He whirled her around to face him, then backhanded her so brutally that her nose broke and began spurting blood. "There will be two sacrifices to the gods this day," his voice boomed out, "an innocent and a whore!"

Jerking her back around to face Vampiri, the high priest shoved Maltheria toward her daughter's draining body and draped her over it so their bodies formed a cross of broken flesh. Sobbing, Maltheria offered her executioner no resistance.

The black skies began to rumble as the high priest turned again to face the crowd. He lifted a sharp dagger high into the air, preparing to offer up the next sacrifice. "I offer unto you…"

Thunder boomed down from the heavens. Lightning pierced the sky.

"The life's blood of…"

The winds began to moan, as if ordering the high priest to cease his unholy incantation.

"This whore…"

The villagers gasped and fell to their knees in fear as the crimson orb in the sky dimmed and the heavens dripped not of life's water, but blood. Malleus' eyes widened in further disbelief as he watched his sister's body slowly rise into a sitting position, her head twisting to the right to regard the unknowing high priest whose back was to her.

"May the gods be well pleased with this unworthy sacrifice and deliver unto us—"

The high priest grunted as he felt an object shoot through his spine and make its way out the other side of his body through his abdomen. Gasping in the throes of agony, he glanced down to his belly and watched disbelievingly as a tiny hand emerged from his flesh and, lurching upwards, sought out his heart. His eyes wide, he cocked his head, swiveling it to see what stood behind him.

The girl. No longer a girl.

"Vampiri!"

Malleus raced up the temple steps toward his mother and sister as the crowd began to scream, his only thought to protect them. He came down on his knees before his sister, staring in disbelief at her surreal image. Her eyes lit up a dull green and her lips parted in a snarl to reveal two sharp, pike-like teeth.

With inhuman strength, Vampiri's fist shot out and punctured the high priest's chest. He gasped as she seized his still-beating heart and wrenched it from his body, snarling as she threw it to the ground like rubbish.

The high priest's gaze clashed momentarily with that of the creature he had unwittingly made. He fell to the ground of the altar, dead.

Malleus wrenched his weeping mother away from the altar and bade her to take to her feet. One glance over his shoulder confirmed his fear that guards were coming. "Stand up, Mother!" he bellowed as the blood from the heavens saturated them all. "Rise up that we might flee!"

Placing Vampiri under one muscled arm and using his other to support his battered mother, Malleus whisked them away from the ziggurat temple as fast as his feet could carry them. They disappeared into the blackened night, Vampiri's mouth wide open all the while to drink of the nourishment the gods had provided for her.

Part I: The Angels Are Weeping

Chapter One
La Spezia, Italy
September 3, 1610

ဆ

"...Mother of God. Pray for us sinners now and at the hour of our death..."

Count Dario Eduardo Giovanni absently handed over his cloak to a passing servant. The sound of mourning, of women weeping as they offered up prayers to the Blessed Virgin Mary, could be heard all the way from the main parlor to the hall where he stood. Curious, he followed the sound as he brushed off stray droplets of rain the cloak had not been able to conceal from the arms of his puffy, full-sleeved tunic.

Upon entering the lavish parlor, which had been decorated with finery from as far away as Persia and Manchuria, the first thing he noticed was that the women weren't the only ones weeping. Even his uncle, a man so stoic Dario had often wondered if he ever felt anything at all, was softly crying as well.

Dario came up behind his mother and gently placed a large hand upon her shoulder. "Mama," he murmured, "*Che è successo?*" *What has happened?*

The dowager countess's head shot up, realizing for the first time that her son had returned early from his business in the port town of Lerici. Placing her hand upon his, she took a deep breath and met his blue gaze so much like her own. "Dario. Dario," she whimpered, "'tis glad I am you have returned…" Eleanora broke down and sobbed, unable to finish whatever it was she had been about to reveal to him.

This wasn't like his mother, Dario thought with a sense of trepidation. She wasn't given to emotional outbursts any more than her brother, his uncle. Eleanora and Paulo had been raised by a cruel man given to tantrums and using his fists against his family. His children had learned to curb their tongues as well as their emotions from an early age.

His gut clenching hotly, Dario rubbed his mother's shoulder in a soothing gesture as he inclined his head to Paulo. He decided if anyone would be able to inform him of what was going on it would be his uncle. His aunt, after all, was wailing as loudly as his mother. "*Zio?*" he asked his uncle. "*Che è successo?*"

Paulo glanced up, meeting Dario's gaze. His eyes were bloodshot from crying. "'Tis your sister," he muttered.

Dario felt as if the breath had been knocked out of him. His eyes widened fractionally—he knew a tragedy had occurred. His uncle of all people would not be crying otherwise. "What is it?" Dario bit out, paradoxically hating the suspense as much as he knew he would hate the enlightenment. "What has befallen Isabella?"

"Oh, Dario," Eleanora cried out as she squeezed his hand. His mother's voice shook as she met his gaze. "*Mia figlia è morta.*"

My daughter is dead.

His mother's words might as well have been a kick to the gut, so devastating they were.

Nay! Dario thought. *There must be a mistake. A huge, ugly mistake.*

"But Mama," the count protested, his own voice doing a bit of shaking, "that makes no sense. She was but training under the countess in Vienna, learning to run a large estate for her betrothed."

This was wrong, Dario thought with a chill of awareness. Certainly a mistake had been made. Young noblewomen did not die learning to do naught more strenuous than playing the flute and making small talk with visiting guests.

Eleanora held up a missive for his inspection. Dario removed his hand from his mother's shoulder and took it. "'Tis written by Elizabeth Bathory's own hand," Eleanora sobbed. "The countess offers me her condolences for Isabella's passing."

Dario swallowed roughly, his eyes misting as he unrolled the missive and read from the parchment. Elizabeth Bathory's penmanship was so flowery and flowing as to seem a mockery to her own words of condolence. Mayhap 'twas his own grief causing him to see things where they weren't, but the feminine scrawl of the countess's hand truly grated just now. It seemed too exuberant, too joyous with energy and vitality.

His nostrils flaring, Dario cursed under his breath as he hurled the missive across the parlor at the Venetian vase atop the fireplace, which shattered as it struck the floor.

Eleanora gasped. "Dario," she said gently, standing up to offer him comfort. "'Tis hard on all of us, my beloved."

"Nay!" he bellowed, shaking off his mother's touch. "Isabella was not so thoughtless as this, Mama. She never, I repeat never, would have wandered from the estate without escort!" Dario's hand balled into a fist.

Let alone been careless enough to fall into a river and impale herself upon jutting rocks.

Paulo stood up with a sigh, his red velvet coat and white garter hose matching the color of his bloodshot eyes. "Dario," he quietly offered, "what reason would the countess have to lie to us, son? She is a noblewoman of the finest breed and well you know this."

"I care not of her breed or recommendation," Dario snarled as he prowled to the other side of the parlor and snatched up the missive he had thrown but moments ago. "This is all lies," he hissed, spacing out each word. "In my heart I know this." His arm flailed about wildly. "Where is Isabella's body?"

Eleanora dabbed at her eyes with a lacy kerchief. Her bosom heaved from beneath the snug fit of her expensive Parisian-made dress as she sucked in a breath and turned speculative eyes toward her son. That quickly she was restored, her usual formidable self. "What would you have us to do, my beloved?"

"Ella!" Paulo bellowed. "'Tis insane to accuse Elizabeth Bathory of—"

"I will travel to Vienna," Dario cut in, keeping the brother and sister from exchanging harsh words. He turned a perceptive eye toward his uncle and waylaid whatever Paulo had been about to say with an upturned palm. "I am not so daft as to accuse anybody of anything without proof, least of all a countess."

Dario's tanned olive features were harsh, determined. His jaw tightened as he regarded his uncle. "But make no mistake, *Zio*, I will find out what truly befell sweet Bella."

Chapter Two
Eisenstadt, Austria
October 5, 1610

❧

Dario sucked in his breath as the bar wench he'd taken up to his rooms at the inn rode up and down the length of his cock. Her large breasts were jiggling, her moans wanton, as her sopping wet flesh enveloped him over and over, again and again. Gritting his teeth, he clutched her hips, his fingers digging into them as he met her movements with deep thrusts of his own.

"Aye," she said breathlessly. "Oh aye." Ersta writhed atop him, plucking at her own nipples to heighten her desire.

Dario's jaw clenched. "Put one in my mouth," he bade her, his thrusts coming faster and deeper.

Leaning over him so that her breasts dangled in front of his face, Ersta shuddered and groaned as he took one plump nipple into his mouth and suckled it. Her breathing grew labored and sporadic as she rode up and down the length of him faster, impaling herself mercilessly, lusty for the need for completion.

Dario found the nub of her flesh with one hand and began rubbing it briskly. He knew exactly what to do to make her feverish for him, knew precisely when to apply more pressure and when to pummel his cock into her depths faster. It was a talent that came naturally to him after many years of practice. He'd lain with more women than even he could count, the two wives who'd widowed him included.

"Mmm," he growled from around her nipple, "'tis a lusty ride you give, sweet Ersta." Finished praising her, Dario's lips curled around the jutting bud again, drawing it back into the warmth of his mouth.

Ersta cried out as she rode him, the pleasure maddening in its intensity. Lips and teeth tugging at her nipple, fingers stroking her clit, a cock buried deep inside her...

"Oh God." Her entire body shuddered and convulsed as she bore down on Dario's iron-hard erection one last time before shattering into orgasm. Blood rushed up to heat her face and her nipples stabbed out as her tummy knotted and she exploded into the most intense climax she'd ever had.

Dario followed soon behind, the contractions of Ersta's flesh sending him over his own pleasure precipice. Releasing her nipple from between his lips, he clutched her hips with either hand and drove himself into her ruthlessly, burying himself fully three times more before he convulsed, coming on a groan.

Ersta smiled down to him as she steadied her breathing. "'Twas a wondrous pokin' ye gave me, milord." She saucily jiggled her breasts for him, pleased when he reached up and cupped them. "I hope ye will give me another afore ye take yer leave."

"Of course," Dario murmured. He smiled into her eyes as he stroked her beautiful pink nipples. They were large and lovely, complementing her fiery red mane of hair. Not as thick as he liked them, but pretty nevertheless. "Where are you from?" he asked idly, noting her accent was not Austrian. "You have the sound of an English wench."

Ersta nodded as she used her hands to rub along the length of the thighs she was straddling. "Aye. I moved here with me mum after Papa died." She shrugged. "Me mum is from these parts."

Dario's mind began to wander to the small journey that still lay ahead of him. 'Twould take mayhap another two days' travel before he arrived in Vienna—and at Elizabeth Bathory's doorstep. It felt like ages since he'd bid his mother goodbye, a lifetime ago since he'd vowed to find out what had happened to sweet Isabella. It felt like ages, but had been a mere two fortnights.

Ersta climbed off Dario and settled herself on an elbow beside him. A thought occurred to him as she clamped her ivory hand around his cock and began to stroke him. "I'm curious…"

"Aye?" She bent her head and flicked at the crown of his manhood with her tongue.

"Are you familiar with Vienna, perchance?"

Ersta answered him between licks as she continued to stroke him into erection. "A bit mayhap, but not very much."

Dario sighed as he ran a hand through his mane of black hair. What was he thinking, contemplating asking a pub wench about the countess as he had been about to do? A woman of Ersta's position in life didn't come into contact with women of the countess' station except to serve them. Even then, servants were expected to be seen and not heard. He knew these things, had grown up knowing them. His only excuse for momentarily forgetting them was that his sister's death was slowly driving him daft.

"Of course," he mumbled aloud, his thoughts straying toward the countess, "I'm sure you've never heard tell of Elizabeth Bathory."

"The c-countess?" Ersta's head bobbed up into Dario's line of vision, her previous task of sucking him erect forgotten. "*That* Elizabeth Bathory?" Her eyes widened. "Tell me ye don't mean her, milord."

Dario's heart stilled. His breathing stopped for a fraction of a moment before he willed himself to breathe. He mustn't give anyone the slightest notion he was here to investigate his sister's death. Not even a pub maid.

Feigning boredom, he raised an eyebrow. "Aye. 'Tis the Countess Bathory of whom I speak." He cleared his throat. "I leave for her estate on the morrow."

Ersta gasped. "Ye don't mean it."

She leaned in closer to him, her eyes wide with fright. Dario could feel her trembling and had to wonder at it.

"'Tis said," Ersta whispered as if afraid the inn walls had ears, "that whenever a wench goes into Bathory grounds, she don't never come back out alive."

Dario felt his insides clenching, his gut knotting. He forced a chuckle to stifle the reaction. "The whispers of ne'er-do-wells and fishwives, like as not."

Ersta looked as if she was about to say something else, then thought better of it. Her eyes shuttering, she turned her attention back to his cock. "'Tis a lusty piece of man flesh ye have, me lord."

Inwardly cursing, Dario plastered a smile on his face. He wanted Ersta to tell him whatever it was she had been about to say. He knew, however, that she wouldn't. Her features had gone purposely blank, indicating she would speak no more on the subject. Not that he could blame the wench. Defaming a noblewoman would, if caught, earn the fiery-headed Ersta a whipping...or worse.

What was important was that Ersta had just confirmed his suspicions. Though the gossip of a commoner would never hold up in court against a countess, it still pointed out to Dario that something was not as it should be. Clearly he had been right to travel to Vienna, to not accept Isabella's death at face value.

He let the subject drop as he lifted his hand to stroke her hair, watching as she licked up and down his stiff penis. "'Tis all for you, my sweet." He sucked in his breath as she took him all the way into her mouth. "Drink up."

* * * * *

Three days later, Dario arrived at Elizabeth Bathory's estate in Vienna a few minutes past the commencement of matins. Handing the reins of his horse over to a stable lad, he brushed off his velvet green cloak and made his way toward the front doors.

He was dressed in the height of Milan fashion today, having concluded that 'twas best the countess realize him to be her equal from their first meeting. He was a count, after all, his rank superior to hers by virtue of his gender.

The outside of the mansion was huge, Dario noted as he glanced about. Resplendent, decadent and lavish. Just what one would expect from a woman of the countess's ilk. Alighting onto the front alcove, he raised his hand to the doorknocker, but was intercepted by a servant before knocking became necessary.

The butler looked him up and down, almost warily. "Milord?" he asked in French.

Dario inclined his head. He spoke back to him in fluent French, a common tongue between them. 'Twas considered the tongue of the civilized and was therefore a language all nobles and their higher servants were versed in. "Bonjour," Dario began, giving him the tale he'd concocted before having left La Spezia, "My name is Count Marco Rossi of Lerici. I am here to see your lady on a matter of great importance."

The butler cleared his throat. He stammered a bit, as if not certain what he should do. Dario thought the action odd, for men of his station were not turned away from anybody's door. Not ever. Not for any reason.

The butler appeared to be considering his options. Finally, with a jerk to his head, he relented. "Of course, milord. Please come in." He shifted his position that Dario might move around him. "The countess is seeing to her toilette, milord. But I shall announce you the moment she adjourns to her parlor."

Dario nodded, but said nothing. He eyed the tall, twisting staircase that led to the floor above, noting the bevy of servants that scurried up and down them to see to their tasks. Odd, that. Most estates of this size boasted a separate hidden staircase for servants to use that their presence might not disrupt guests. "*D'accord,*" he murmured his assent.

The butler led Dario into a guest parlor, taking his outer robe before offering him a refreshment. Their conversation continued in French. "Would you care for a goblet of wine, milord, or a tankard of ale mayhap?"

"Wine would be welcomed. From a white grape if you have it."

"Of course, milord." The butler inclined his head, preparing to make his exit. "My name is Hans if you've the need of me. I'll be but a moment with the wine. The countess received a new shipment from the Tuscany valley a sennight past. It should make you feel right at home."

Dario nodded. "My thanks." He watched the butler turn on his heel to leave, then stopped him before he could reach the doors. "Hans?"

The servant turned around, his eyes wary again. "Aye, milord?"

"The staircase..." Dario's eyes squinted almost imperceptibly. There was a puzzle piece here that didn't quite fit and he disliked anything he couldn't make sense of. Actually there were several puzzle pieces that didn't fit, including the bizarre fact that every one of the many servants he'd seen going up or coming down the stairs had either been male or an old woman. Not a young maiden amongst the entire lot.

Still, he couldn't ask too many questions all at once. He couldn't be so obvious. "Why do the servants not use the back staircase?"

"Oh that," Hans said too quickly, his gaze averted. "'Tis nothing, milord. The countess's bathing chamber rests above the back staircase and milady wishes no interruptions during her toilette."

Dario stifled the urge to raise an eyebrow. He schooled his features into a fashionably bored mask as he considered another oddity that had just been placed before him.

Hans had said that the countess took her toilette in her bathing chamber. Most bathing chambers were part and parcel of the bedchamber itself, if even such a separate room existed.

"I was but curious," Dario said dismissively as if the butler's answer hadn't been the least bit significant. "I look forward to the wine."

Dario watched the servant take his leave, noting before Hans turned that beads of sweat had broken out on the old man's forehead. Another oddity.

And as the expensive timepiece down the hall chimed loudly to let all and sundry know matins had passed, the most curiously jagged piece of the puzzle yet clicked in his mind. During the hour when most pious noblewomen would be saying their prayers at chapel, Elizabeth Bathory was seeing to her toilette.

Dario's gaze flicked toward the ceiling. In that moment he realized he could not and would not leave Vienna without first inspecting the inside of the countess's bathing chamber.

* * * * *

Elizabeth Bathory was everything and nothing like Dario had presumed she would be. He had expected to find the countess a self-absorbed and vain woman, pretentious and worldly in her airs. And she was—she was all those things and more.

He had not expected, however, for Elizabeth Bathory to be the most stunningly beautiful and excitingly sensual creature he'd ever laid eyes on.

It was rumored that the countess was nearing two score and ten years, but Dario found the notion hard to credit. The woman sitting across from him at table in the dining hall looked to be a score and five if she was a day.

Her long black hair, which she'd left to flow wantonly about her shoulders rather than securing it into a properly modest bun at her nape, hadn't any hints of gray. It was shiny and looked satiny to the touch with a vitality about it that only young maidens tended to possess.

The countess' skin was yet further testament to youth, to a visage the hands of time had been unable to mar. She was possessed of creamy porcelain skin, flawless and without wrinkles. Even when she smiled, as she was doing now whilst raising a goblet of wine to her lips, not one line about the eyes could be discerned.

And her teeth, Dario noted as she flashed a seductive grin his way, her teeth were pristine white, so white they damn near gleamed. Not at all the half-rotted teeth of a woman reaching her fiftieth year.

Either the rumors had been wrong and the countess was much younger than the society gossips had whispered her to be, or Elizabeth Bathory had discovered the secret elixir of eternal beauty, the mythical location of the fountain of youth. A man ruled by reason and logic, Dario decided it was the former.

"I've never had the occasion to travel to Italy, Marco..." The countess broke off and, with another of those seductive grins, regarded him from across the dining table. "I realize we've just met, but I already feel as though I know you." Her creamy bosom heaved from above the inappropriately low-cut bodice of red silk she wore. "Do you mind terribly much if I call you Marco?" she murmured.

Dario smiled slowly, one corner of his mouth tilting upwards. "Who am I to stand upon ceremony?" he asked softly, the look he gave her blatant in its suggestiveness.

He knew the countess wanted him, which didn't surprise him in the least. Dario wasn't given to vanities or to strutting about like a court peacock, but neither was he prone toward false modesty. Women had always wanted him. Ever since the age of ten and five when he had shot up to his current six-foot-three stature and his body had begun to bulge in all the right places, he had been considered an ideal catch. Add into that mix the title and lands he'd come into at a score and two and he'd become every society wench's dream knight in shining armor.

"Excellent," the countess said, her voice low and throaty, "and I bid you to call me Elizabeth."

"Elizabeth it is then."

Dario's gaze clashed with the countess's and held. Her dark eyes appeared to be assessing him, no doubt sizing up his worthiness as a lover. That, he reminded himself, was just as well.

In truth, the thought of making love with the very woman who might have had a hand in Isabella's death disgusted and repulsed him as nothing else could, but his feelings toward the beautiful—and no doubt cunning—Elizabeth Bathory were irrelevant. He would gain her confidence. He would gain her trust. And he would do it in the most expedient manner possible—by bedding her.

"I daresay," Dario began after sipping from his goblet of wine, "you speak remarkable Italian for a woman who has never had the occasion to visit my homeland."

Elizabeth sipped slowly from her goblet, both hands cupped around the base. Her dark eyes found his blue ones from over the rim as she drank, then with a measured ease she withdrew the bejeweled chalice and set it atop the polished oak table. Before she finished swallowing, a droplet of red wine began to trickle slowly from the crease at the side of her mouth.

The color of the wine droplet was so red as to be startling. Dario could only wonder at what manner of grape could produce so vivid a red. But before he could ask, Elizabeth's tongue darted out and lapped it up from the crease at her mouth.

"I've never before visited the Italians in all their glory, 'tis true…" Her smile was slow, her eyes glazed over with passion. "But I didn't say the Italians had never come…to me."

Dario felt his penis stiffen at her suggestive words and hated himself for it. An irony, mayhap, since his plan was coming along quite admirably thus far. The countess had, in effect, just offered him the use of her body. She had all but declared herself a wanton with her over-the-top words.

By meal's end, his tongue would be shoved down her throat. Fifteen minutes later, his cock would be plunging into her. But for now, he conceded, 'twas best to reaffirm his alleged reason for having shown up at her doorstep to begin with.

He smiled, letting her know her innuendo had been received and would be acted upon. "And to think," Dario said drolly, his eyes twinkling, "that I had almost sent a missive at my aunt's bequest rather than taking the time to stop off here myself."

The countess chuckled, a guttural, unsettling sound. 'Twas the only aspect of her that felt quite…wrong. His stomach clenched and knotted, but he ignored the odd reaction.

"Please inform your aunt that I would dearly enjoy taking her daughter under my wing so to speak." Her black gaze became intense. "How old did you say she was, Marco dearest?"

"Two and ten."

"Such a wondrous age," she murmured. "So young, so vibrant and full of life. So innocent…"

Dario smiled as he listened to Elizabeth prattle on, the odd feeling in his stomach growing more pronounced. They had been dining together for over an hour and until the past few minutes most of the conversation had revolved around his "niece" and her need for a tutor in the wifely skills of running a large estate. And now, after having flirted for barely five minutes, the conversation had once more reverted back to his mythical niece. If the countess's incessant nostalgia with the subject was any indication, the topic was a personal obsession of hers.

What, he asked himself uneasily, was this fascination she had with youth, and with young girls specifically? And why, he wondered as his stomach knotted impossibly tighter, did he harbor no doubts but that this bizarre obsession of the countess's had something to do with Isabella's death?

Dario stood up, his gaze never leaving the countess's. He knew exactly what to do to seduce a wanton like Elizabeth and he would waste no more time in seeing to it.

She ceased speaking as she watched him leave his seat. Slowly, in measured footfalls, he made his way next to her and looked down to her from where she was seated.

"And when," Dario murmured as he stood directly to the side of her chair, "was the last time an Italian came...*in* you?"

Elizabeth's breath caught in the back of her throat. She glanced from his face down to the obvious bulge of his erection, noticeable through the hose he wore. She lifted her hand and, glancing back up to his face, began stroking him through the fabric. "A lifetime ago, Marco," she whispered.

Dario sucked in his breath, torn between arousal from her touch, self-loathing that he could get hard for her and disbelief that she was stroking him in the middle of the dining hall for any passing servant to see. "Then by all means, Elizabeth," he replied in thick tones, "let me remedy that for you."

Her obsidian gaze sharpened a thousandfold, the intensity startling. "Do you wish to belong to me, handsome Marco?" she murmured.

A chill of foreboding trickled down Dario's spine. The question was odd, very odd. 'Twas simply not the sort of query a woman put to a man, and most definitely not a man known to her for all of an hour's time.

Something about Elizabeth Bathory was wrong, he knew—very wrong. So wrong that 'twas making panic set in, making beads of sweat break out on his forehead, and inducing his heart rate to accelerate in an unnatural manner.

Dario pushed aside the portentous feelings he was experiencing and concentrated on the countess. Knowing what had truly become of sweet, trusting Isabella was all that was important.

He leaned into her palm, giving her the full effect of his erection. "Aye," he said softly.

Part II: The Dead Walk Amongst Us

Chapter Three

✍

Dario's watchful gaze took in everything as Elizabeth led him from the dining hall on the ground floor to her bedchamber on the second rise. There was nothing remarkable about his observations, he thought with a certain amount of disappointment — nothing appeared other than as it should be.

But then what had he expected? For all the answers surrounding Isabella's death to make themselves known the moment he commenced his first stroll through the mansion?

'Twould take patience. Skill at ferreting out the answers and an ungodly amount of patience in procuring them.

"Here we are, handsome Marco," Elizabeth purred, coming to a halt before her bedchamber door. She licked her lips and glanced suggestively down to his crotch before looking back to his face. "I daresay you are the finest gentleman I've ever had the pleasure of welcoming into my lair."

Your lair?

He met her black gaze and feigned a lust he did not feel. He almost slipped and bade her to call him "Dario", his true name, then recalled the lie he'd concocted before arriving at her decadent, bizarre world.

Here, he was Count Marco Rossi of Lerici. He'd never heard tell of a Count Dario Giovanni of La Spezia. Until he knew what had truly befallen his beloved sister, Lady Isabella of La Spezia, 'twould be the way of it.

"And you," Dario murmured, one strong hand coming up to brush back a lock of her black hair, "are the most sensual, beautiful woman I've ever seen."

Her eyes, once wanton, flashed back to the honed, overly keen look they'd taken on back in the dining parlor. Her gaze brought to mind a hungry bird preparing to swoop down from the heavens and snatch up a tasty field mouse.

Everything about the wench was odd.

"Once you enter my bedchamber, there is no going back." The countess made her invitation for sex sound like a lifetime commitment. "Are you certain you wish to belong to me?"

Long enough to search your estate and question your servants.

"Aye," Dario said thickly.

Her gaze blurred, reverting to its lust-drunk visage. A creamy, porcelain-white hand found the doorknob.

"Come with me," she whispered.

Dario took a deep breath and gently expelled it as Elizabeth opened the large, double doors to her massive bedchamber. He felt like a whore for hire, not wanting to perform sexually for the very wench he believed had a hand in his sister's death, yet desirous of the potential results such a union could bring. Namely, her trust—and with it, answers. Casting his reservations to the wayside, he followed the countess inside her boudoir.

Dario stilled, unable to believe the sight that greeted him.

The bedchamber, eerie in its décor, resembled a dungeon of torment more than a serene place of rest. Shackles and manacles lined the walls, as did other implements of torture. His stomach rolled when he espied fresh stains on the stone walls, stains he knew were the remnants of spilled blood.

Dario looked away. He had thought to behave as though naught was amiss, but there was no concealing his shock and revulsion.

"What is this place?" Dario rasped, his blue eyes disbelieving as his gaze flew to the countess.

You are evil beyond comprehension.

Countess Elizabeth Bathory was more than an eccentric, more than a mysterious, reclusive beauty who ran a household where young wenches like Isabella curiously disappeared. She was the devil incarnate inhabiting a woman's skin.

Her lips parted into a slow, wide smile. Two of her teeth protruded like pikes.

Dario blinked, wondering if she'd put something in his wine that would cause him to hallucinate. The countess was mayhap many things—vile, sadistic, cruel—but a vampire she was not. Such creatures were naught but fables, lurid imaginings of the feeble-minded and lack-witted.

"'Tis a place like no other," Elizabeth said throatily. "A place where life meets death…and conquers it."

Her words were a puzzle, yet Dario found himself lacking the patience to piece them together. The rage he'd fought so hard to conceal burst to the surface in a flare of temper.

"You are mad!" he spat, one arm flinging wildly toward the bloodstained walls. "What goes on here?"

She was unmoved, unworried, about his change in demeanor. The wench needed to be locked away in an asylum—or any place where she could cause no more pain and suffering to innocents.

Dario had never struck a woman in his life. 'Twas discomfiting to admit he wanted to slap her, hard. 'Twas even more repulsive to realize she would mayhap enjoy it.

"Calm thyself," Elizabeth instructed him. She motioned toward the other side of the bedchamber, over to a gaggle of naked wenches he hadn't even realized were here. "Pleasure unlike that which you have ever known awaits you, milord."

The countess met his furious gaze. He found himself staring into her eyes, a bizarre calm instantly enveloping and transfixing him. His muscles, once tense, seemed to relax in a heartbeat. 'Twas as if he'd been mesmerized, the inexplicable experience akin to a snake he'd once witnessed a charmer entrance during his travels.

What in the name of all that was holy was happening to him?

"Relax," the countess softly commanded.

Both his body and his mind responded. Mayhap his mind was deceiving him, yet he could have sworn she flashed him those two dagger-like teeth again.

"Soon you will belong to me, Dario. I take good care of mine own."

From somewhere in the back of his clouded brain, he realized she had said his true name. Had he slipped and spoken it? Or had she known who he was all the while, mayhap even expected his inevitable arrival?

He battled against the drugged calm that ensorcelled him. 'Twas a vain effort.

Beautiful, naked wenches surrounded him. They led him toward the countess's massive bed, undressing him as they walked. Dario felt as if he were living in a dream, unable to understand what was happening, unable to control the situation or its outcome. Elizabeth, naked too, pushed him down onto the plush covers, her nipples standing stiff as she hovered over him.

"My pets will prepare you for me, handsome Dario," Elizabeth purred.

Pets? Surely she didn't mean—

In the blink of an eye, wenches were all over him—young, beautiful, big-breasted wantons who looked more than eager to pleasure him. There had to be ten or more of them, their tempting bodies and undeniable lust making his unwilling cock go rigid.

'Twas a dream and no more, a figment of his overly virile Italian mind. There was no other explanation. Naught else made a wit of sense.

A sexy blonde wench grabbed Dario's cock by the root and squeezed. She smiled at him sinfully, then licked her lips before enveloping the whole of his cock into her throat. He hissed as she sucked him hard, the pleasure unbearable.

And then there was another mouth. And another, and another. They kissed, licked and sucked him everywhere, leaving no part of his body in neglect.

'Twas but a dream. It had to be. Mayhap he was still lying abed with Ersta, a nightmare the likes of which he couldn't have conceived devouring him whole. And yet the hands, the mouths, the teeth...

They felt so real.

An exquisitely built redhead lowered her pussy down onto Dario's mouth. He groaned as his tongue instinctively darted out. She rode his face for endless minutes, soft, breathy gasps expelling from her throat as she repeatedly rubbed her hole and clit over his tongue in rapid, successive movements.

His hands, balled into fists, found soft breasts on either side of him. Dario could see nothing save the wet, hot pussy sliding over his mouth, but he could feel the breasts of two more wenches at his hands. He grabbed the soft globes as the redhead continued to ride his face, pulling and tweaking at every stiff nipple his ravenous fingers could find. The wenches moaned in response, and Dario couldn't help but to become further aroused by knowing he was bringing three women to climax simultaneously.

The blonde attending to his cock sucked him harder, faster. He groaned into the redhead's pussy, every muscle in his body tensing. The wench riding his face moaned and came, and Dario all but spent right then.

The redhead dismounted. The blonde released his cock from her mouth with a popping sound. Elizabeth Bathory took over, straddling him, situating the entrance of her flesh near the head of his cock.

"So thick and long," the countess praised. Her eyes shuttered, kohl-black lashes fanning down. The two pike-like teeth gleamed. "And so mine."

Dario warred with himself from the back of his fevered mind, struggling to resist her overwhelming, ethereal allure. And yet his head was filled with sensual cobwebs, unable to concentrate on anyone or anything save the perfect, youthful, naked body preparing to fuck him.

His soul was cold, his body was on fire.

Elizabeth sat astride him, long hair the color of the darkest night falling down to a narrow waist and lush hips. Her large breasts were firm, her pink nipples stiff and extended, as though she'd never aged a day past twenty. An inverted triangle of black curls pointed to her pussy hole.

Dario's heart had never wanted a woman less; his cock had never desired a woman more.

"What," he rasped, perspiration soaking his forehead, "are you doing to me?"

She smiled that devil's grin of hers, the daggerlike teeth protruding prominently.

He could no longer deny what the countess was. Nor could he do a damned thing to save himself from whatever fate she had in store for him. Dario could only pray to the saints that death was his providence—quick and preferably merciful.

You must live. Sweet Isabella must be avenged.

The thought sustained him. 'Twas the only piece of his true self that permeated the sensual, drugged haze Elizabeth had engulfed him with.

The countess grabbed Dario's penis by the root and ran the head over her clit. Purring, she situated his cock at the entrance to her flesh and impaled herself with a growl.

Her brown eyes flashed green, white teeth jutting impossibly further out, before throwing her head back and riding him. Many feminine hands caressed him all over, further arousing him whilst their mistress fucked him.

Moaning, Elizabeth rode him hard, her big tits jiggling with every downstroke. The sound of skin slapping against skin, of pussy suctioning in cock, resonated throughout the stone chamber. She rode him harder and faster, her fingernails digging into his chest.

"Come in me," Countess Bathory commanded on a gasp, "*Now.*"

Dario's teeth gritted, his mind wanting to resist succumbing to orgasm, his body unable to do anything but. She wielded a power over his person that was frightening and inexplicable in its intensity.

His entire body stiffened, then convulsed on a loud, reverberating groan. Dario shot a strong stream of cum into her womb, the orgasm long and violent.

Breathing heavily, his eyes barely open, the last thing the count saw was an acute green gaze hovering over him and two sharp teeth baring. He closed his eyes and roared as the fangs tore into the flesh of his neck, then convulsed again with a second climax so ruthless it put the first one to shame.

He could feel the blackness coming, knew that he was losing consciousness. The final thought he would ever entertain as a human was a startling revelation.

Vampires were real.

And Dario was now one of them.

Chapter Four

ဢ

"Wake up, milord," a male voice beseeched him in whispered French. "Before it's too late for your sister."

Isabella? She's still alive?

Dario groaned, his eyelids so heavy they felt held down by stone weights. He wanted naught more than to do as the voice pleaded, yet he couldn't seem to rouse himself no matter how hard he tried.

Memories assaulted him. Haunting images of his blood being drunk...and of him drinking of the countess's. Sex all night with so many wenches. His cum inside them all, blood exchanged betwixt the lot of them.

Sweet Mother Mary.

"Wake up!"

The voice was louder, more insistent and somehow familiar. The man was careful to keep his voice a hush, but the resolve in it could not be mistaken.

"Please...you *must* awaken."

Is it you, Hans?

It took all his effort, but Dario managed to force his eyes open long enough to ascertain that, indeed, 'twas Elizabeth's butler who hovered over him. Sunlight bore into Dario's eyes, eliciting a painful hiss from the depths of his throat. He threw his hands over his face to shield them.

"I know it hurts, but you can still walk in the light. Wake up, milord. 'Tis Lady Isabella's only chance."

Was the butler a vampire too? Nay. His scent was distinctly human. Dario could smell his blood, could hear it pulse within his mortal veins.

What in the name of God is wrong with me?

Isabella. His beloved innocent of a sister. He had to help her. No matter the pain, he needed to awaken.

Forcing his eyes open from behind his hands, he slowly permitted the sunlight to penetrate them. He cried out from the maddening pain it caused, raged against whatever illness was within him until he conquered it. It took long minutes, and the pain never completely subsided, but at last he could look upon Hans without his eyes burning as though salt had been thrown in them.

"What has become of me?" Dario demanded, his voice gravelly. "Tell me!"

"*Shhhh*," the butler chastised, helping Dario to stand. The Italian count was as weak as a babe. "Keep your voice down lest you rouse the countess. I will tell you all that I know, but you must keep your silence until we are gone from here."

He wasn't accustomed to taking orders from anyone, yet Dario had no choice but to acquiesce to Hans' dictates. Something incomprehensible had occurred last eve, an evil that still permeated the very chamber he had awoken in. Leaving the vile room behind wasn't a hardship.

"I will follow where you lead," Dario panted. Talking was difficult. Walking was a vastly greater effort. "But you best have answers."

"You won't want them once they are revealed to you, milord," Hans predicted. He propped Dario up and gave him his shoulder to lean on. "But I will tell you all that I know."

* * * * *

Had Dario not experienced yestereve's nightmare for himself, Hans' tale would have been too incredible to believe. The butler looked to be nearing three score and ten, yet he claimed the countess was much, much older than he.

"My sire served her, as did his sire before him. I've no notion how old she truly is. All that I know, milord, is *what* she is."

A vampire—a vicious creature that preyed on humans and killed without remorse or pity. Dario had thought vampires a fantasy, the sort of mythical monsters peasants warned their children of to keep them in hand.

Not so mythical after all.

The sound of a neighing horse broke Dario from his silent reverie. He blinked, the pain in his eyes not nearly so overpowering as when he'd first awakened, but present nonetheless.

"You have served her the whole of your life?"

"Aye, milord."

"Why are you helping me?" he rasped. "Surely you must know the countess will punish you."

The old man said nothing. He had been trapped in Elizabeth's sordid, evil world since birth, death his only possible escape.

The hair at the nape of Dario's neck stirred as he regarded the bone-weary butler. Hans could withstand no more; the old man didn't care if he lived or died.

"She is most powerful after darkness falls," Hans explained, ignoring the question Dario had put to him, "yet she is able to walk amongst the living in the sun. She cannot abide the sunlight for long spells, though. An hour at most, mayhap a bit longer."

Dario thought of every vampire myth he'd ever heard tell of. Minute details changed from storyteller to storyteller, but one thing always remained the same. Sunlight killed vampires.

"How is she able to endure the sun?" Dario asked. He closed his eyes, tiredly resting his head against a horse's stall. The truth of his own fate hit him in the gut, hard. "And how am I for that matter?" he murmured.

The butler seemed to sigh. "You will not be able to walk amongst the living in daylight hours for o'erlong, milord. I do not understand the why of it, yet I know from years of experience that it takes mayhap a sennight before you fully become one of them. After that time, you will sleep as the sun rises and awaken as it sets."

A week. That was all he had left. One short sennight and he'd never be able to feel the delightful heat of the sun kiss his face again.

In seven days, he would be a monster.

"And the countess?" Dario asked, his eyes opening to regard the butler. "How does she walk in the sun?"

"She spills the blood of innocents," Hans answered softly, "and drinks it."

Dario's stomach lurched. "You have seen this?"

"Aye."

His nostrils flared. Rage engulfed him, renewing his energy. He no longer gave a damn about the sunlight that burned his eyes. "Isabella? Was that what became of my sister?" His jaw clenched in fury. "She was naught but a lamb for slaughter?"

Hans nodded. "Her and countless others, milord."

Callous, mayhap it was, but the others didn't concern him at the moment. Isabella did.

"Where is her body?" Dario grated. He needed to see it, needed to sob over it. 'Twould give him the strength to kill Elizabeth Bathory with his own hands. "*Tell me.*"

Dario's gaze seared the butler's. He instantly recalled the words Hans had used to rouse him from his drugged slumber.

Wake up, milord. Before it's too late for your sister.

His blue eyes widened. It took all of his effort, but he managed to drag himself to his feet. His breathing was heavy, and he felt as if he were dragging a two-ton rock along on his back, but he made his way from the back of the stables to where he could stare at the grand, twisted stone estate of the Countess of Bathory. Hans followed on his heels. "Does Isabella still live?" he panted.

"Aye, milord. Barely. But she still has a chance."

Dario cocked his head and locked gazes with the old man.

"The countess was so absorbed in you last eve that she didn't have time to drink from one of her prisoners before the sun took to rising…"

A dark eyebrow slowly inched up.

"She cannot walk in the sun without ingesting the spilled blood of a female virgin," Hans reminded him. "So long as there is sunlight, you have a chance to free Lady Isabella."

Silence ensued as the two men stared at each other. Dario's mind raced.

"How can I kill your mistress?" the count asked quietly.

Hans handed him two coins. Dario palmed them and stared curiously at the copper things. He'd never seen anything like them. They looked to be old, ancient in fact. But what could they possibly have to do with—

"You will need those later. Do not lose them."

Dario inclined his head as he watched the old man walk across the stable. Hans kicked away hay and strewn leaves, then knelt to the ground and threw open a revealed secret door.

"The countess never sleeps in the same place twice," Hans informed him. The butler nodded for Dario to follow. He picked up four wooden stakes and handed two of them to Dario. "And we've only got four hours more to find her."

Chapter Five

ഌ

The world Hans led Dario into was a nightmare from which there was no awakening. He could feel the hand of death touch him, grip him. Worse, a sense of homecoming encompassed him too.

'Twas a vile place. A cold, underground cemetery filled with coffins, spiders and rodents. And, of course, vampires.

The tombstones were tall and lavish, each one like its own mausoleum. There were at least thirty of them, three long rows of crypts filled with the sleeping undead. He could see the massiveness of the graveyard even before the butler lit a torch.

The old man's eyes were that of a human's. Dario's were not.

"She could be in any of them," Hans muttered. "We must search them all, milord."

In four hours, and in Dario's weakened condition?

The fact that the sunlight didn't penetrate at all down here didn't seem to signify. 'Twas as if he were a programmed animal, his body instinctively knowing 'twas the hour of rest. He raged against the drugged feeling, forcing his gaze to sharpen.

He wasn't fully one of them. Not yet. 'Twas, mayhap, the only advantage Dario currently wielded. And even then, an advantage that would die as soon as the sun set.

"I won't pretend to know all there is to know of this clandestine society," Hans said as he withdrew a skeleton key and opened up the first tomb. The door creaked on its hinges, obviously quite old. "But I do know that only another vampire can kill a queen."

"A queen?"

The butler shrugged. "'Tis how I think of the undead, milord. The countess is like the queen of a colony of bees. 'Tis nigh unto impossible for a human to kill her. She is too ancient, too strong. Only one of her drones can end her reign of death. And even then, only when all the cards are played right."

This eve, the cards could be played right. Dario hadn't turned enough yet to be completely helpless during the sun's reign. The countess had neglected to drink of a virgin's blood before sunrise. Surely Hans had been awaiting such an oversight on his mistress's part for decades. Indeed, the old butler went about opening the first tomb with strength and determination a man half his age would be hard-pressed to summon.

"Hurry," Hans instructed the count. "Every moment that ticks by brings us, and thereby Lady Isabella, closer to death."

A chill swept over Dario. Somehow, Elizabeth knew they were here and why they had come.

And she was indomitably trying to muster the strength to stop them.

In the darkness, the Countess of Bathory possessed any number of minions that would see to her bidding. In the daylight, she had but one sentry. And he had turned against her.

Dario walked over to the first crypt and entered it. Hans motioned to a trapdoor inside the small place.

A tomb inside a tomb. The search could take forever.

"We must kill every creature we encounter," Dario commanded as they followed a dirt path that led down further into the earth's belly. "They have been under the countess' spell far too long and will kill us to protect her do we not kill them first."

Dario wasn't certain how he knew that, but he did. And he cursed Elizabeth Bathory for it.

They seemed to walk forever, naught but dirt and the occasional rodent to be seen. The lower they went, the chillier the air became. For all the biblical talk of hell's heat, Dario decided death was cold. And terribly lonely.

"There's the first one," Hans murmured, using the hand that didn't hold the torch to point westward. "Over there."

Dario's eyes widened when he counted not one, not two, but seven, coffins. He looked questioningly at the butler.

"Each crypt houses seven, milord," he answered, seeing the question in the count's gaze. "As I said, we've much to accomplish before sunset."

Seven vampires in every tomb. Thirty tombs. Over two hundred vampires.

A bit of an understatement.

Dario's heart picked up in tempo as they approached the first coffin. The creature knew what was about to happen and was helpless to resist its fate. That smothering knowledge caused Dario's heart to wrench, no matter that his victim was a vampire.

Hans hoisted the coffin open. A male lay there, eyes closed and palms folded across his chest. Even in sleep, his hands had been positioned to protect his heart.

"Move its hands," Dario instructed Hans. He held up a wooden pike, preparing to impale the vampire's heart. "*Now.*"

The butler stilled, his face showing the first signs of fear. "Aye, milord."

Hans hesitated for another moment, then slowly reached out to do Dario's bidding. His own hand shook as he moved one of the male vampire's hands and positioned it next to one side of its body in the coffin. Dario could hear the butler breathe in relief when the creature failed to retaliate.

"And now the other," Dario murmured.

A bead of perspiration trickled down Hans' forehead. The old man knew he had to move that hand because it was covering the vampire's heart. Dario could only wonder at what horrors Hans had witnessed over the years for he could smell his fear.

Dario raised the wooden stake above his head, two strong arms ready to lash down and impale. "The clock is ticking," he reminded him. "Move its hand."

Hans seemed to hold his breath as he slowly, hesitantly, reached for the second hand. He grabbed the creature's wrist and nervously moved it next to the other side of its body. The butler took a quick step back.

The vampire's eyes flew open, their lit-up green searing Dario with hatred. The creature hissed, revealing two protruding incisors.

Jaw clenching, blood pounding, Dario drove the stake through the vampire's heart. Their intense gazes clashed as the vampire grasped the wooden pike with two weak hands. It screamed, the death cry shrill and ear-piercing. The repulsive sound vaguely reminded the count of a newly born babe wailing for milk.

Dario's teeth gritted as he twisted and ground the stake into the vampire's heart. The unholy wailing continued until, at long last, its eyes dulled and its hands fell limp.

Breathing heavily, Dario stared down at the creature, twisting and grinding the stake, making certain it was dead. He felt sick, revolted by the fact that *this* was what he would become. Gazing upon the vampire—its eyes, its teeth, its dead soul—'twas like glimpsing into his own stark future through a looking-glass.

"It's dead," Hans said softly, a gentle hand resting on Dario's shoulder. "Milord…please."

Dario blinked. Panting, he withdrew the stake from the vampire's heart and closed the coffin. The blood coating the wooden pike was black, not red. Sweet saints.

Hans said nothing, though he was certain the butler could see the anguish writ all over his face. But then what could

Hans possibly say to him? Naught could change what Dario was becoming.

The Italian count would murder the Viennese countess. And then he would kill himself.

"We can speak of you and your future later," Hans reminded him. "We've much work left to us, milord."

Dario closed his eyes and took a deep breath. One vampire dead, two hundred and nine left to vanquish.

Thankfully, mercifully, killing the undead became easier with each rotting corpse the two men left behind. Indeed, they all but had their system down to an art. Dario opened the coffins, Hans moved their positioned hands and Dario struck.

When three hours and some minutes had passed and they'd killed nigh unto two hundred vampires, the count began to worry that they might not find Elizabeth's resting place until 'twas far too late. There were two tombs left— fourteen undead creatures.

And mere minutes until sunset.

"We must work fast," Dario instructed, entering the next crypt with Hans. "Time works against us now."

"It always has, milord."

As sunset approached, Dario grew stronger, more powerful. Unfortunately, he knew the same would be true of Elizabeth. The count wielded but two advantages over the countess—his ability to walk in the sun and his dogged determination to save his sister.

He prayed to the saints 'twould be enough.

They killed another vampire. And another. And another. She was everywhere and she was nowhere. Dario could feel her, could smell her, and yet she continued to elude him.

The men alighted from the second to the last tomb and back up into the dark, cold underground cemetery. Their gazes both wandered to the final crypt. The countess of Bathory had to be in one of the coffins deep below it. There was nowhere else left for the vampiress to lie in wait.

Hans clutched a crucifix and, holding it to his lips, kissed the feet of his God. Pocketing the religious symbol, the butler pulled out the skeleton key and prepared to open the vault.

The key sank in. The door did not open.

The old man fumbled with the key, eyes rounding. "It won't unlock," he gasped, his terror tangible.

Dario checked his pocket watch. Eleven minutes to sunset.

The count could feel the queen vampiress pushing against the door to the crypt with her mind. 'Twas as if she possessed an ethereal key on the other side of it, quickly locking it every time Hans unlocked it.

Nine minutes to sunset.

"Nay!" Dario bellowed, muscles tensing, fury erupting. They could not have come this far only to lose now. "You will not win!" he roared, hammering against the sealed tomb door with his fists. He kicked at it, beat it with his shoulder. "Damn you to hell!"

The door to the crypt flew open, slapping Hans in the face with its brute force. The old man slumped over, eyes rolling to the back of his head, his body falling to the ground. Elizabeth Bathory stood over him, eyes lit up green, pike-like teeth revealed.

"When I go to hell," the countess vowed, "I take you with me."

She attacked him with a speed and force the likes of which Dario could not have imagined. The countess slapped him, hard, whirling Dario ten feet across the cemetery as though he weighed no more than a leaf.

Fury engulfed him. Rage overtook him. Something inside him snapped, as two deadly fangs ripped from his gums. His green gaze clashed with hers and narrowed.

The vampires fought long and ruthlessly, sounds erupting from their throats that bespoke of two animals fighting to the death. Elizabeth ripped at the flesh of his neck with her teeth. Dario cried out, falling, yet managed to hold onto her, taking her to the dirt ground with him.

They wrestled for control — the ancient vampiress and the newly turning creature who had only rage and the dwindling sun on his side. She pounded him with her fists, clawed at him with her nails, yet somehow amidst the pain, Dario managed to climb on top of her, wresting control for a flickering moment.

He couldn't win.

The thought hit him like a deathblow.

Elizabeth was the very queen Hans had warned him of. She was ancient, possessing power he couldn't begin to fathom. The sun was sinking. Time had run out.

Dario held Elizabeth's hands over her head even as he knew she would soon overpower him. The evil wench smiled up at him, toying with him, letting him hold her down before she killed him.

"You are a fool," the countess taunted, "a damned — "

Her eyes rounded on a bloodcurdling scream. Exhausted, Dario panted from atop her, watching in disbelief as a wooden stake sank into her heart.

Hans. The butler wasn't dead after all.

Teeth gritting, Dario added his own weight into the mix. He twisted and ground the stake deeper and deeper into her heart as the countess gurgled, black blood oozing from her mouth.

It seemed like forever but was mayhap only moments before her eyes unlit, her mouth closed and she lay upon the dirt ground.

"The coins," Hans reminded him. "Place them over her eyes, milord."

His breathing heavy, Dario did as the butler bade. He had no idea what the coins signified, but realized Hans' knowledge of this world was greater than his own.

A copper coin rested on each of her eyes. Dario stood up over her corpse and stared down at her.

"We'll seal them with hot wax after we kill the others," Hans said. "'Twill keep her from awakening for eternity."

A curious black eyebrow arched.

"A stake isn't enough for a queen or a king," Hans told him.

Dario glanced at his pocket watch. Two minutes until sunset. Six vampires left. He could question the butler later. Right now they had more kills to make.

"Let's go," Dario gasped, forcing himself to enter the stone crypt. The fight with the countess had stolen his strength, but he was determined to finish the job he and Hans had set out to do. "And then take me to my sister."

Chapter Six

ဆာ

Dario would never forget the horror that was the Countess of Bathory's bathing chamber. A bevy of young female virgins strewn along the stone walls — tied down, naked and very close to death. The count fell to his knees and sobbed when he espied his beloved Isabella.

His sister, so good and thoughtful of others, so kind and quick to laugh, had been tied to an inverted cross, gashes all over her innocent body. Chairs had been positioned all around her, partially-drunk goblets of blood scattered about.

Dario could well envision the torture little Isabella had endured these past weeks. Vampires surrounding her, laughing and jesting with each other as they slashed at her body and poured themselves a drink. To them, she had been naught more than a feast they kept alive as long as possible, that they might indulge in her over and over again.

"Bella," Dario rasped, his eyes bloodshot from crying, "Bella, I am here."

She was weak, nigh unto dead, but she heard him. A faint smile crossed her lips. "I knew you would come," she whispered.

* * * * *

It took months for Isabella's body to heal and years for her spirit to mend. Mayhap she would never fully recover, but Dario was with her through it all. After freeing the other young wenches he returned her to La Spezia, reuniting her with their elated family.

Hans had elected to remain behind in Vienna long enough to make certain that the countess was buried far away from civilization, in a place where no one would ever find her and unearth her remains. When his duty was done, he would sail to Italy and remain with the Giovannis for the remainder of his mortal years.

Somehow, unthinkable as it was, Dario was able to shield that which he had become from his family. Except, of course, Isabella. His sister protected him fiercely, going so far as to convince their mother that Dario had acquired an illness in Vienna that made him so tired all the time. 'Twas why he slept the whole of the day.

Lady Eleanora never knew that he prowled the nights, taking blood where he could. Dario never killed the humans he drank of. Nor did he ever make one into what he was.

Twelve years later, on a cold December morn, their mother passed away in her sleep. Dario wept over her body, Isabella and her husband of ten years at his side.

Time came and went. His family members grew old and, alas, died. Dario never aged. None in Isabella's family ever questioned him, though he suspected that, as time went on, they understood.

A plague swept the countryside years later and Isabella lost everyone—her husband, her children and her grandchildren. She was seventy and seven and the pain was simply too much for her to endure.

Dario begged her to hold on, to rage against death, for she was all that he had left in this world. He even offered her the unthinkable—eternal mortality—that she would stay with him, not leave him behind.

Lady Isabella, now possessed of silver hair and wrinkled skin, smiled up to her elder brother, an inhuman man who didn't look a day past thirty and five. "I love you, Dario," she whispered, her voice tired and aged. "Because of your sacrifice, I led a long, happy, full life."

She was ready to die. Tears welled in his blue eyes as he clasped her feeble hand.

"Bella," he said softly, his voice cracking, "please do not leave me alone."

"My husband and children await me on the other side," she told him, her love for him shining in her eyes. "Your destiny lies in this world. Mine does not."

"I have no destiny," Dario rasped.

"God never makes a mistake," Isabella said softly. "He let you become that which you are for a reason. You must find what it is."

Dario smiled down at his sister, tears gently rolling down his cheeks. "I will miss you so much, Bella. I will never forget you."

"I love you, Dario. Always."

She closed her eyes and died as he held her hand. Dario wept, his body shaking with the ruthlessness of it.

Sweet Bella was gone. And Dario was very alone.

* * * * *

Years came and went—cold, lonely decades spent in isolation. Dario had naught but memories to sustain him. He visited the graves of his family often, seeing to their upkeep. Isabella had been dead for nigh unto fifty years, yet he recalled her smile as though they'd laughed together only yestereve.

Ironic though it was for a vampire, Dario's most cherished time was during sunlight hours. When he slept, he oft dreamt of an elusive, beautiful wench with flaxen hair and a dimpled smile. She dressed oddly, in clothes that made little sense to him.

She was his everything in those precious hours he had to dream. He could smell her, taste her, nigh unto feel her. Like a phantom just out of arm's reach, she promised him happiness, an end to the stark loneliness…then disappointed him with her nonexistence every eve when he awoke.

He wanted to die — the one thing he could not do.

Other than servants and the occasional paid whore, Dario had no contact with people, except for those he drank of. Years pressed on and the outside world slowly changed with the passage of time. It became neither better nor worse, only different.

And still, she was there, smiling that dimpled smile whilst he slumbered, tempting him with her feminine beauty and carnal allure. Dario ached to hold her, to breathe in her scent, to sink his cock deep inside her.

She wasn't real. She would never be real.

Isabella had once spoken to him of destiny. Dario didn't need a fortune-teller to understand his.

He had been cursed to walk alone, a shadow in alleyways during the darkest nights.

Part III: The Evil Has Risen

Chapter Seven
Iraq – former Mesopotamia
Present day

ဢ

"You're so lovely – so beautiful."

She blushed and looked away. "No, I'm not."

His fingers, strong and insistent, found her jaw. He forced her to look up at him, yet she couldn't see him. She never could.

"I've waited so long for you," he murmured, his deep voice like a caress. The reverberating sound worked its way down her spine, beckoning to her. "So damned long…"

The daydream was always the same. A man – tall and powerfully built. He came to her in the daylight hours, summoning her to him. Although she'd never seen what he looked like, she sensed that he was handsome. And sad.

And terribly in love with her.

Blinking several times in rapid succession, Dr. Dawn Miller snapped out of the trancelike state that had momentarily engulfed her. Her mind had entertained many similar, bizarre daydreams lately. She didn't know what to make of them, but conceded that since they only occurred while she was awake, they were probably due to lack of sleep.

"This is crazy," she mumbled under her breath as she wound her way through the gravesite. She'd worry about catching up on her rest later. "I don't have time for a mental meltdown right now."

Wearing faded blue jeans, a white T-shirt and her long blonde hair secured in a ponytail, Dawn took to her knees on the dirt and studied the corpse she and the other archeologists had just unearthed. All thoughts of the daydream immediately scattered, her focus on her work. Her forehead wrinkled in concentration as she stared down at the bodily remains.

A thirty-five-year-old American scientist with over a decade of site digs under her belt, Dawn took less than a minute to realize their team was dealing with an oddity. All the other graves they'd dug up were inhabited by Mesopotamian people who had died somewhere around ten thousand years ago, but this female corpse wasn't nearly as old.

"What do you think?" murmured her British colleague, Dr. Jerry Weston. "She's very well-preserved. I'm baffled."

So was Dawn. "She was young when she was murdered." The puncture wound in her chest and defensive wounds on her arms suggested she'd put up quite a struggle with her assailant. "Look at her teeth—not a bit of decay."

"Early twenties?"

"Maybe younger, but that sounds about right."

"The year of death?"

Dawn laughed quietly as she stood up. "I'm not Nostradamus," she mused. "We'll have to run some more tests and bring in someone more familiar with period clothing, but my guestimation is…ohhh…1500s to 1600s, maybe?"

What the hell was a European woman doing buried here amongst peoples who had died thousands of years before her? It made no sense.

Jerry nodded. "That's what I was thinking too. But you're right—we need a confirmation."

"It's odd, though, isn't it?" Dawn asked softly.

"Hmm?"

An elusive thought just out of reach continued to evade her, so she focused on the one thing that she could put into words. "The coins sealed over her eyes."

"What do you mean?"

"We've found a lot of Mesopotamian graves where the dead were buried with coins sealed over their eyes, but I've never heard of this rite being performed on any people beyond the B.C. years."

"Me neither. And that's what makes her intriguing."

"Those coins look Mesopotamian in origin."

"More intriguing still."

"We'll have to remove the coins carefully so we can test them to make certain." Dawn brushed the dirt from her jeans and motioned for Jerry to follow her. "After lunch." She flashed him a dimpled grin. "I'm starving."

She hadn't slept in two days, but putting off the tests didn't so much as occur to Dawn. She was more than a consummate professional — she was a woman who relished her work. Fascinated by ancient ruins and long-dead cultures since the tender age of eight when her father took her on one of his digs, she had never wanted any other lifestyle than the one she possessed.

"I don't know how you can be so bloody cheerful on so little sleep," Jerry grumbled, following Dawn to the gravesite. "It's obscene."

Dawn held up a lantern, smiling as they walked. He was as excited to run the tests as she was, and they both knew it.

"I'm still a young and agile thirty-five while you're an old man of thirty-seven," she quipped. "I've got a couple of good years left in me."

"You'll be young and agile at eighty-five. You're obnoxious like that."

She chuckled as they passed four Iraqi guards and entered the secured site. "My father was tireless until his dying day. Hopefully you're right and it's in the genes."

"Send me a postcard in thirty years and let me know. You'll find me and my wife sipping margaritas at the beach, having long ago retired to the south of Spain."

"Liar."

Jerry winked at her but said nothing.

The two scientists weaved their way through grave after grave until they arrived at the one they were most interested in. The tomb had been secured inside a tent, lanterns illuminating the area encompassing it. A Yale University anthropologist that they both knew, Dr. Linda Kine, greeted them.

"You got here quickly," Dawn said, hugging her. "Thanks."

"Don't I always?" The older doctor smiled, laugh lines crinkling at the corners of her gray eyes. "I may be officially retired, but I wasn't about to pass up an opportunity to see this. I'm glad I didn't."

Dr. Miller looked at Linda quizzically.

"You were right, Dawn," Dr. Kine confirmed. She stared down at the preserved remains of the young female they'd dug up earlier in the day. "Her clothing was of the noble class and distinctly late 1500s to early 1600s in fashion. But that isn't what boggles me."

"What do you mean?" Jerry asked.

"Well," Dr. Kine sighed, "her clothing is at odds with the era in which she lived. Very bizarre."

Dawn's brown eyes widened in rapt attention as she listened to Dr. Kine's fascinating analysis. A world-renowned scientist in her field, the seventy-two-year-old Linda had retired four years ago but was still lured back to the field when an anthropologist of her expertise was required.

"I'm not sure I follow," Dawn said. "What are you getting at?"

"She's much older than you think," Linda explained. "Probably three hundred years older."

Silence ensued as the other two scientists absorbed what they'd just been told. A chill worked its way up and down Dawn's spine as she stared at the lifeless, mysterious corpse lying in the ground.

So well preserved as to be confounding, the woman had clearly been beautiful in her heyday. Long dark hair, alabaster skin, full, crimson lips...

The only telltale signs of death were her lack of a pulse and the emaciation that had ravaged her body.

"So we have a female born in roughly the 1300s, dressed in period costume that can be placed in the late 1500s to early 1600s, whose eyes have been sealed shut by what we presume to be two ancient coins from around 7000 to maybe 8000 B.C." Dawn blew out a breath, trying to make heads or tails of the situation. "Have I missed anything?"

"I bloody well need a drink," Jerry muttered. "You missed that."

"None of it makes sense to me either," Linda admitted. Her expression was one of perplexed concentration. "Are you certain the coins are Mesopotamian?"

Dawn shook her head. "No. I need to run more tests."

"You do that." Linda patted her on the back. "Jerry and I can stay here and guard the countess."

"Countess?" Jerry mused. "You know this for a fact?"

"No."

"Then..."

Dr. Kine shrugged. "We're a week away from Halloween, she's dressed like a vampire of lore and it's obvious from the puncture wound through where her heart would have been that somebody believed she was the real deal when they murdered her."

Jerry snorted. "Countess Dracula, eh?"

"Well, we have to name her *something.*"

Dawn ignored her colleagues' banter and reflected on what Linda had just said about vampires. It nailed that funny feeling she'd been carrying around all day right on the head.

The young noblewoman's murderer *had* thought she was a vampire. It explained a lot, namely why the area in the chest cavity that had once contained her heart had been pulverized. Like an innocent burned at the stake during the Salem Witch Trials, the deceased female had been branded a heretic and slaughtered. Poor girl.

Some important pieces of the puzzle had come together in Dawn's mind. Now if only the clothing made sense. And the coins…

She and Jerry had been trying to figure out that mystery since they dug up the ancient remains of the first corpse they'd found buried in a similar fashion. Adrenaline coursed through her veins. This was why Dr. Miller loved her job with the passion she did. So many riddles to solve.

"If you two will help me remove the coins from her eyes as carefully as possible," Dawn interjected, "then I'll go run the tests and see what I come up with."

"Will do," Linda said.

"I can't wait to hear your results, Dawn." Jerry rubbed his hands together like a kid anticipating the arrival of Santa Claus. "Countess Dracula is the best find we've had in a long, long time."

Dr. Miller smiled at her two friends and colleagues. An ominous feeling she couldn't name swamped her senses.

Shaking it off, she leaned over the corpse, preparing to remove the coins. It would take a bit of work as whoever buried the young lady's body had all but fused them to her eyelids. "Well," she said, pulling on a pair of latex gloves, "there's no time like the present."

* * * * *

"Jackpot," Dawn whispered to the mobile lab's walls. Her pulse picked up as she eyed the coins under the microscope. "These babies are at least ten thousand years old."

It was an important find. The ancient people who had once inhabited the Zagros foothills of modern Iraq had been far more advanced than historians thought. Despite similar Mesopotamian coins she and Jerry had unearthed in previous digs, scientists had still credited the Lydians for inventing the first ones.

Clearly, archeologists had been wrong. And now Dawn could prove it. There was no mistaking the well-preserved details that had been painstakingly etched with crude tools into the copper coins. The ancient Mesopotamians had known how to mine and manipulate metals thousands of years before the Lydian empire existed.

But how had the countess's murderer known about the coins? What significance had they held to him or her?

Excited, confused and giddy all at once, Dawn carefully slid the two coins into an airtight bag and slipped them into her jeans pocket. Jumping out of the RV, she slammed its door shut and ran as fast as her feet would carry her back to the gravesite.

Finally—finally!—they had their proof. Jerry would be as elated as she was.

Pulse pounding and her breathing ragged with exhilaration, Dawn burst into the tent. "You guys aren't going to believe this! I can barely believe it myse—"

She came to an abrupt halt. She blinked, her eyes unable to trust the sight that greeted her. It couldn't be.

It was.

"Oh my God," Dawn gasped, instinctively taking a step back as her eyes widened in shock and horror. Her heart threatened to beat out of her chest. "*Ohmygodohmygodohmygod.*"

An arm lay here, a torso there. Blood was spattered everywhere. Insects and small rodents were already assembling, dining on the meat of the carcasses. A vile stench filled the tent. Nausea churned in Dawn's belly.

At first it was hard to make out who the victims were, but then she spotted the severed heads. "No!" Dawn cried out, backing away from the grisly scene. Linda and Jerry had been butchered, slaughtered like pigs. "This isn't happening!" Her horrified gaze flew to the grave the tent had been erected around.

The body was gone.

She whirled around, noticing the dead Iraqi soldiers on the far side of the tent for the first time. In her excitement to share her findings with the other scientists, it had escaped Dawn's notice that the guards weren't stationed where they were supposed to be.

Her head began to spin, her mind to splinter. Like a deer caught in headlights, she couldn't move, could barely breathe.

The sound of a low, sinister growl reverberated through the tent, breaking the spell. In fight-or-flight pattern, her head immediately cocked to the right.

Dawn struggled for breath as her gaze clashed with a lit-up green one. It couldn't be her...not *her*! She watched in disbelief as the dead woman smiled, revealing two pike-like fangs.

"You're dead," Dawn whispered, unable to look away. Her throat was dry, her lips parched. "You aren't real."

The emaciated female stared at Dr. Miller with a hatred so intense it sent goose bumps zinging down her spine. The creature wanted to kill her, but for some reason didn't. Its bony hand balled in frustration, then let loose on a roar against Dawn's cheek.

The powerful blow managed to hurl Dawn out of the tent and three graves away. The impact was so jarring she realized she was losing consciousness. She wanted to scream, to crawl away with what little strength she had left, but there was no going anywhere.

Dawn struggled not to vomit as her stomach churned and dizziness assaulted her. Five seconds later, her battered body slumped to the ground and she knew no more.

* * * * *

"Milord? Milord, are you ill?"

Dario gasped as he struggled to regain his footing. Elizabeth's awakening had been the strongest, most abhorrent feeling he'd ever known. Hundreds of years had passed by and many things had changed—technology, clothing, even language—but one thing would always remain the same. His hatred of the countess.

She had killed already. He could feel it in his gut, knew it with every fiber of his being.

She had to be stopped. This time forever.

"Milord? Please speak to me."

Dario's blue gaze flew to the only mortal who knew what he was. His trusted butler and friend these past twenty years, there was nothing about Count Giovanni that Piero did not know.

"Milord?"

"She has risen," Dario murmured, perspiration soaking his hairline. Speech was difficult. His voice was raspy, determined. "Someone has awoken her."

Chapter Eight
Six weeks later

෨

Dawn was beginning to wonder if they were right. Maybe she was insane. Lord knew there was no other explanation that made a lick of sense.

"I didn't say you're crazy," Dr. Andrews, her university-appointed psychiatrist, clarified. "I said that I think you suffered a temporary insanity which was brought on by the duress of the extreme circumstances you found yourself faced with. Insanity isn't something that a person can just 'snap out of', but a temporary insanity is. What happened to your mind in those awful minutes could have happened to *anyone*, Dr. Miller. You need to understand that."

She wanted to. She really did. But the memories, the nightmares—they were still so real.

A month and a half had ticked by, yet every time she closed her eyes she saw that lit-up green gaze and emaciated face staring back at her, watching her. Those eyes haunted her every nightmare. If Dawn had imagined it, then why wouldn't the creature go away? She put the question to the psychiatrist.

"Your brain became confused," Dr. Andrews logically replied. "It's very common."

"But—"

"Think about it, Dawn. Realistically. Like a scientist. Step away from the situation and analyze the horror of that night with that eagle-sharp mind of yours."

Dawn ran two punishing hands through her long blonde hair and sighed. Dr. Andrews was right and there was no getting around it. Vampires were make-believe. Whatever had happened that night, a human had done it. Unfortunately, it looked like she, he or they would be getting away with it, too.

"Dr. Kine had named the missing corpse Countess Dracula right before she was murdered," Dawn whispered, recalling that fact for the first time since the massacre.

"You see!" Dr. Andrews spread her hands. "Proof positive."

"What do you mean?"

"Just minutes before the trauma occurred, the suggestion of vampirism had been fed to your subconscious. When the real terror began, your brain became confused, unable to separate reality from fantasy."

Dawn had to admit her explanation made a great deal of sense. Dr. Andrews' impeccable reputation was the reason Dawn's superiors at Harvard had insisted she get counseled by her to begin with. Dawn sagged in relief, not totally convinced the psychiatrist's words were true, but convinced enough to feel a huge weight lifted from her shoulders.

"Take a vacation," Dr. Andrews suggested with a smile. "You've earned one, and what's more, you need one."

"But the investigation—"

"Will carry on just fine without you." Dr. Andrews nodded definitively, then clasped her hands together atop her oak desk. "The authorities have your mobile number should they need to reach you. Your memories will come back when they're ready and not a second earlier. In the meantime, you, my dear, need some rest and relaxation."

Dawn slowly inclined her head. On that they were agreed. She just hoped that getting away from everything would actually help.

Ever since the night Linda and Jerry were murdered, Dawn had felt scared, vulnerable and unable to sleep for more than a few minutes at a time. Living alone was hard on the nerves during such a crisis, but she refused to cave in to the emotional weakness and ask a friend to spend the night. If she did, one night would turn into two, two into three, and before she knew it, she'd be a dependent, fragile shell of her former self. Not acceptable.

"It's cold and wintry here in Cambridge," Dr. Andrews pointed out. "Why not go somewhere warm and sunny?"

Weather wasn't an issue. Dawn would go dogsledding in the Arctic if she thought it would make the nightmares stop. "Thanks," she said noncommittally, standing up. She was tired of talking about that horrible night. The need to escape the situation engulfed her. Hoisting her duffel bag over her shoulder, she paused long enough to flash Dr. Andrews a brief hint of a smile. "I'm not sure where I'll go, but I'll figure something out."

* * * * *

Dario hadn't laid eyes on Vienna in four hundred years. He had hoped to never see it again. But this was where Elizabeth would come. No matter that her home was now a museum — to her it would always be her possession.

Over the years, historians had written of Elizabeth as the depraved serial killer that she was. They believed her to have been mentally ill, though biographies written of her life often hinted at her "acts of vampirism" and "obsession with eternal youth". None of the writers truly believed that the countess had been a creature of the night, but keeping her ghoulish legend alive sold entry tickets to her home and kept the museum financially sound.

Fools. They would never know — could never know — the full truth behind the sick shrine that Elizabeth's mansion had become.

"What an honor it is to have you as a guest in Hotel Sacher, Count Giovanni." The reception manager inclined his head respectfully. "We trust you will enjoy your accommodations during your stay in Vienna."

Like many Old-World European villages, much of Vienna had changed since the Renaissance and much of it had also remained the same. The hotel was new — at least to Dario. A tavern had sat here in its stead some four hundred years ago.

"Yes. I trust that I will."

The dawn was coming and Dario's body protested it. He needed shelter from the sun — immediately.

Accepting the key to his chamber from the reception manager, the count doggedly made his way to the presidential suite. Having given the hotelier strict instructions that he was not to be disturbed for any reason whatsoever, Dario thrust open the double doors to his room and pulled all the drapes closed, thankful they were heavy and thereby impenetrable to the sun's rays. That accomplished, he all but fell into a heap on the bed.

Hands folded protectively over his chest, Dario succumbed to deep slumber. His dream woman had eluded him for weeks, but today she made her presence known. She was scared, frightened and not at all her usual self. The fact that she was not real didn't signify. Dario ached to protect her, to comfort her.

To make her feel secure in a world devoid of safety.

* * * * *

"Do not be afraid, little one. I will allow no harm to come to you."

"I wish you were real. I need you."

His powerful arms drew her in close to his chest. She could hear the steady beat of his heart, feel the security that only his embrace could provide.

Why couldn't he be real?

"I am real," he said softly. "You are the phantom, bella..."

Dawn blinked. She blinked again. *Bella.* The word was Italian for "beautiful".

Her daydreams were crazy. *She* was crazy.

On a deep sigh, Dawn plopped down onto her bed in Hotel Sacher and stared at the ceiling. Why had she come to Vienna? She had never possessed even the tiniest desire to see it, yet for unfathomable reasons had been irresistibly drawn to it.

Her gaze flicked to the nightstand beside her bed, and to a bunch of tour brochures that lay there. Sitting up, she plunked the pile of pamphlets onto her lap and leafed through them.

Freud's house — boring. Vienna coffeehouse tour. Huh. Just what she needed — more caffeine to keep her impossibly more awake than she already was. Vienna Zoo. Schönbrunn Palace tour. Haunted mansion of the Blood Countess. Opera House. The —

Dawn's gaze flew back to the tour of the haunted mansion. Her pulse picked up for inexplicable reasons as she thumbed over to page nine for an in-depth description.

Countess Elizabeth Bathory, known to antiquity as the "Blood Countess", was murdered in the early 1600s by unknown persons who believed her to be a vampire. Whether human or monster, Countess Bathory was undeniably responsible for the torture and murder of hundreds of servant girls and perhaps a dozen or more children of the noble class. Rumored to be obsessed with eternal youth, she purportedly believed she could obtain it by drinking her victims' blood. Was she a vampire or merely a twisted sociopath? Come see the house of horrors that is the Bathory estate and draw your own conclusion.

We provide tours in many languages, including English, Japanese…

Dawn stopped reading the description and quickly scanned the page for when the next English-speaking tour was scheduled. Her heartbeat quickened as she located the information she sought.

"Tonight," she whispered to the walls.

Maybe she was crazy. Maybe she was trying to put together a puzzle that didn't exist. Maybe Dr. Andrews—and everyone else, for that matter—was right.

And maybe, Dawn thought as she fell back onto the bed with a sigh, maybe she could let her obsessions go after she visited this Blood Countess' home...and realized once and for all that vampires didn't exist.

Chapter Nine

ಬ

The moment the tour bus rounded the corner and Countess Elizabeth Bathory's mansion came into view, Dawn began feeling nervous. The estate was palatial, atypically grand for the area, even for aristocratic homes built during the Renaissance. The moon hovered just above the grounds, illuminating the front doors and iron-wrought gates while concealing nearly everything else.

"It's a full moon tonight," the tour guide announced in a thick Austrian accent. Obviously well-rehearsed at this, she widened her eyes as she gazed at the crowd. "They say the Blood Countess comes back from the grave on nights like this one."

Elementary school-aged kids looked up at their parents through frightened eyes. Teenagers goaded each other and giggled. The adults grinned, getting into the mood the tour guide was setting impressively well.

Dawn swallowed roughly as the motor coach pulled through the front gates. Her heart dropped into her stomach. It didn't escape her notice that she felt as on edge as the little kids did.

Stop it! Pull yourself together, Dr. Miller.

"Are you ready?" the tour guide asked in hushed tones.

"Yes!" the teenagers shouted in unison.

"Then let's go inside."

Dawn closed her eyes and took a deep breath. Her brown eyes flicking open, she waited for the passengers in front of her to disembark before standing up and following.

Sliding her hands into her jeans pockets, she stared at the entrance to the countess's house with wary, watchful eyes. The closer the group got to the doors, the worse she felt. Nausea, headache, dizziness — she didn't know what was wrong.

Probably another panic attack. She'd had a few of them since that awful night six weeks ago.

"Ladies and gentlemen," the tour guide announced, her fearful expression pasted on, "welcome to the home of Elizabeth Bathory — the Blood Countess!"

* * * * *

Dressed in black trousers and a black silk shirt, Dario easily blended into the shadows. He watched with the honed eyes of his kind as the tour group made their way to the front doors of the mansion. A woman with long blonde hair walked determinedly up the steps, something about the way she moved sparking a sense of déjà vu. Her back was to him, so looking at her face wasn't an option. Yet there was something about her...

She wasn't Elizabeth — that was for certain. Firstly, the vampiress was a brunette and, secondly, the mortal woman radiated a goodness that the countess wasn't capable of. He stared after the stranger until she was well out of sight, then forced himself to shrug off the bizarre feeling.

He had to find Elizabeth. Now. Before any more atrocities were committed at her hands.

She had killed many times since her awakening, leaving a trail of corpses across Eastern Europe. The media blamed the sudden surge of murders on a serial killer. They could never know who and what the true killer was.

Dario had met a few more of his breed over the centuries. Not many, but enough to realize that most vampires were like him rather than Elizabeth. They drank from humans but didn't kill them. They sought only enough blood to survive, and they kept to themselves.

Very unlike the countess.

Eventually, just as Dario had predicted, the serial killer had moved toward Vienna, leaving a path of dead, mutilated female bodies drained of blood in her wake. She was here now, somewhere within the grand estate. Finding her before she preyed upon the tourists was of utmost concern.

This was Elizabeth's home. She wouldn't take kindly to strangers traipsing through it.

He could smell her, feel her—knew she was here. She had taken in much virgin blood over the past six weeks, growing stronger and more powerful every night. Soon, if she was not stopped, she would begin rebuilding her army of protectors. Dario could not allow that to happen.

Count Giovanni had learned many things about vampires in the centuries since he had become one. At the time Elizabeth was laid to rest, he and Hans had known of only one mechanism through which to keep the undead dead—the ancient coins. Cremating her body hadn't so much as occurred to them.

It had taken four hundred years, but Dario would finally finish what he had started. There was no other choice.

His beloved sister, Isabella, had once spoken to him of destinies. Perhaps protecting the mortal world from the likes of Elizabeth Bathory was his.

"Follow me up the back stairwell," the tour guide directed, "and next we will see the bathing chamber of the Blood Countess." She began ascending the staircase, her voice loud enough to be heard, but hushed enough to stay dramatic. "It's a vile, evil place. This is where most of Elizabeth Bathory's victims died...after they'd been tortured for weeks."

Dawn frowned at all the giddy excitement the tour guide was generating amongst the crowd. It occurred to her that people were strange, and oftentimes their own worst enemies. There was nothing to feel invigorated about when it came to visiting a room where so many young girls had been viciously murdered. Such a horrible circumstance of history commanded a respect that time — even four centuries' worth of it — shouldn't mar.

The crowd was corralled into the large bathing chamber, the doors to the room shut firmly behind them. Dawn gazed around. The place sent chills up and down her spine. Stone walls. Bloodstains...

The crowd gasped. One little boy began to cry. Dawn's head swerved to the left. She couldn't see what had everyone so disturbed — she was too far back in the swirl of people — but she could hear their collective fright and upset.

A knot of tension coiled in her belly. Something told her to get to the front of the crowd, to find out what the hell was going on.

Dawn pushed her way through the throng, her heartbeat further accelerating with each step. Children were crying, grown men looked ready to faint.

And then she was there, standing at the front of the crowd, her eyes unable to believe what it was she was seeing. It couldn't be — *it couldn't*.

It was.

"What is going on?" the tour guide whispered to her aide. "Nobody told me there was to be any sort of reenactment here tonight."

"I don't know," her British aide answered, as perplexed as she. His voice sounded worried. "But I don't like this."

Two teenage girls from the tour group had been chained to the walls, their clothing torn. Almost naked, the girls were crying, terrified, their eyes round and faces pale. The crowd gaped at them like deer caught in headlights, not certain what was happening, why it was happening or who was the cause.

Dawn knew. She saw her — *it* — standing off to the side.

The dead woman her psychiatrist had tried to convince her was still dead.

A lit-up green gaze clashed with a horrified brown one. The vampiress snarled at Dawn, revealing her fangs. The crowd, finally noticing the intruder, recoiled. They had no way of realizing just who it was they were staring at—that she was the real Blood Countess.

Monsters weren't supposed to be real.

Elizabeth Bathory made a move toward the chained-up girls. The teenagers began to cry. Dawn moved quickly, instinctively, bodily shielding them so that the countess couldn't touch them.

"Get back!" Dawn shouted, her heart threatening to beat out of her chest. "Don't touch them!"

Elizabeth's nostrils flared. Her hand balled into a fist of frustration at her side.

In that moment the truth hit Dawn like a bullet between the eyes. The creature couldn't kill her. She could hurt her, even slap her out of the way again, but she couldn't kill her. Dawn was like a persistent gnat to the countess, a disease that she couldn't make go away.

Finally, another piece of the puzzle came together. All these weeks Dr. Miller had wondered why her life had been spared while everyone else's had been extinguished. Now it all made sense.

Dawn was the one who had removed the coins from the vampiress's eyes. *She* was responsible for awakening her.

Guilt mingled with determination coursed through Dawn's veins. Thinking quickly, she picked up a nearby candlestick and maintained her defensive position in front of the teenage girls. The creature's eyes narrowed at her, and Dawn knew she was about to strike.

She had to think—fast. There was no other human alive who was capable of protecting the kids from the Blood Countess. If Elizabeth knocked Dawn into unconsciousness again, the girls were dead.

The creature moved toward her. Dawn's pulse skyrocketed. Beads of perspiration dripped from her hairline.

She was no match for a vampire. Not even for the one she was responsible for awakening.

On a deafening roar, Elizabeth was hurled against a wall. Dawn blinked, her brain fighting to keep up with what her eyes were taking in.

A big man, very tall and muscular. His hair was dark, his eyes the same lit-up green as the countess's. Dressed from head to toe in black, he moved with surreal speed as he attacked the countess. The sounds the two vampires emitted during the violent struggle brought to mind animals fighting for dominance.

Oh my God. Another one?

Her pulse skyrocketed. Dawn didn't know who to root for. The one who couldn't kill her but was intent on trying, or the one who probably could kill her but seemed more interested in killing the countess.

The crowd began to laugh and cheer. Dawn's eyes widened as she looked back at them.

"Get her!" one man shouted.

"Kill her!" another added.

"Yeah! All right!" screamed a third.

They thought this was staged. They believed they were watching two actors pummel each other for their viewing pleasure.

Dawn's gaze flew to the teenagers behind her. Even they had calmed, hesitant smiles forming on their faces.

Dawn went with it. Anything to spare the two kids from the nightmares she'd been plagued with since that horrible night in Iraq six weeks ago.

Ignoring her own fright, Dawn's eyes searched the room for the key to the shackles that bound the kids. It felt like forever but was less than a minute when she at last espied it sitting on a chair near where the vampires were engaged in battle. Moving hurriedly, she sidestepped the skirmish and reached for the key.

Elizabeth's hand, no longer emaciated, clamped down on top of hers. Dawn's face drained of color.

He was there again, the mysterious vampire who radiated a hatred for the countess that ran deep, deeper even than Dawn's own. Grabbing Elizabeth by the wrist, he broke her hold on Dawn, freeing her. She swiped up the key and ran.

Undoing their shackles, Dawn yelled at the girls—and then at the crowd—to go. They clapped and whistled, making her teeth grit. Her brown eyes bore into the tour guide's, letting her know she was serious.

The tour guide nodded, her eyes round. She had to know this was no reenactment.

"We have to leave now!" the tour guide shouted, hustling everyone out of the bathing chamber. She threw her assistant a worried look. "I thank our hosts for an amazing night and now we must return to the bus!"

Amidst groans of disappointment, the crowd followed her. Dawn sagged in relief as she watched them exit.

"*Cet fois, tu mourras!*" the male vampire raged in a language she didn't understand. "*Le monde en a assez de toi!*"

Elizabeth slapped him hard, knocking him backward. He rebounded quickly, flying toward her, taking her down to the ground.

Dawn's feet felt cemented to the floor, her eyes glued to the grisly brawl. She needed to run, to hide, to get away from the countess long enough to figure out how to put her back to sleep. Hopefully the male vampire would take care of the last, but then who was to take care of him?

She hadn't awoken the male. She was completely defenseless against him.

The male's head turned, cocking to look at Dawn. Their gazes clashed and held. He stared at her with a hunger, an intensity she couldn't name. It chilled her to the bone. Then his blue eyes did something enigmatic to her, forced her to surrender to a calm and peace that was completely at odds with the situation.

Dawn swallowed roughly, still uncertain if he meant to harm her or not. Her heart said no while her mind screamed yes. Rational logic won out.

The male vampire had to know she was aware that he was real, that he and his kind weren't make-believe. He had to want her out of the picture, unable to carry her tales to other humans.

She blinked, breaking his mesmerizing stare. Unable to think of anything but escaping, Dawn turned and ran from the scene, fleeing to the tour bus and away from the Bathory estate.

Chapter Ten

ဆ

Elizabeth managed to escape.

Dario had no one but himself to blame. He had been so lamentably close to ending the countess's mad reign there and then, but he'd been taken off guard.

He hadn't expected to see *her* here tonight. He hadn't even thought she was real.

The phantom lover from his dreams, the mortal woman who had haunted him for centuries — hundreds of years before she was even born.

He would know that face anywhere, would recognize that flaxen hair, those amazingly sexy brown eyes and full red lips, out of a million women who possessed the same attributes. Every fiber of his being had burst alive upon seeing her. His rage had known no bounds when he realized Elizabeth was about to attack her.

She feared him, the nameless woman who had kept his sanity intact throughout the past four hundred years. He couldn't blame her really. Were their positions reversed, he would have felt the same.

Dario's muscles corded as he made his way through the forest. He didn't sense Elizabeth's presence and wasn't certain where to look for her. He would have to bide his time, for now — until he got a lock on her scent again.

The dawn was coming. He needed to seek shelter from the sun immediately.

He shapeshifted into hawk form, something that had taken him half a century to perfect. Dario took off into the predawn, the imminent arrival of the sun a call to sleep for all nocturnal creatures. Tomorrow night he would find the human woman.

Elizabeth's scent was eluding him. His phantom lover's wasn't.

* * * * *

"What is your name, bella?"

"Dawn."

"Dawn. Very beautiful – just like you."

When she spoke her name it sounded quite ordinary. When he spoke it, it sounded anything but.

"My name is Dario. Count Dario Giovanni."

"A count? How apropos."

He seemed amused. "I've read the stories of the other count. Fiction, more like than not."

She smiled. "But Vlad the Impaler – Count Dracula – was real."

"True. But since I've never made his acquaintance, I will assume he was bloodthirsty in the warring sense, not the literal sense."

Dawn was enjoying the inane banter. She went quiet when she realized that fact, her emotions in chaos. A long quiet ensued.

"There's little point in running from me, bella." Dario's chuckle was gentle, like a caress. "Now that I know you are real, I intend to keep you."

"You want to kill me."

"Never." His tone turned harsh at the accusation. "Not all of us are like Elizabeth, little one. Not all of us are monsters."

She wanted to believe him. "Then what are you?" she whispered.

"I don't know. Perhaps you can help me find out."

"You want…to make me like you."

Silence.

Her teeth began to chatter. She had no desire to drink blood from humans for all of eternity, as though they were mere cattle providing milk for her sustenance.

"I would never force you," he murmured. She couldn't see him. Why was it that she could never see him in her daydreams? "I wouldn't force my will upon you."

She sensed his sadness, his resignation – his loneliness. Her heart ached to tell him she would make certain he never had to walk alone again, but she wasn't the type of woman to make promises she couldn't keep.

Dawn blinked, coming out of the trancelike state. The man of her daydreams... It couldn't be him. *He* wasn't real. He had been a nightmare – or a daymare – *something*. And now he was a daymare with a name.

Count Dario Giovanni.

She paced back and forth in her hotel room, uncertain what to do or how to feel. At least she could put her fear of insanity to rest now that she knew vampires were real – the only boon from an otherwise terrifying night. Still, sanity or lack thereof aside, that left a lot of other problems. Namely the two vampires that now knew of her existence.

Elizabeth was frightening enough, but the male – yes, the man from her daydreams – *God*. No man had ever looked at her like Dario had back at the Bathory estate. Those smoldering eyes had revealed many emotions in one simple stare, sensations that confused an already mind-boggling situation.

Dominance. Possessiveness. Need. Determination. Yearning...

She ran both hands through her hair as her teeth sank into her lower lip. His reaction to her was unfathomable. But then, her reaction to him had made even less sense.

It was his voice, she decided. Something in it calmed her, gentled her fears and erased her worries. His voice was authoritative, commanding respect. And yet so damned gentle when he came to her in the daytime.

"This is crazy," Dawn muttered to herself. He had obviously mesmerized her, or whatever it was his kind did. "I've got to get out of here."

She hastily packed her suitcase, not knowing where she would go or what she would do, but knowing she had only until sunset to figure everything out. She had to hunt Elizabeth.

Even as the immortal Italian count hunted Dawn.

* * * * *

He awoke at sundown on a roar, nostrils flaring, fangs exploding from his gums. Sweat drenched his face, his chest, as he shapeshifted back into the all-seeing hawk.

His dream lover — Dawn — had run from him.

The primal part of his brain, the piece that recognized his mate when he saw her, couldn't stand for it. All thoughts of Elizabeth fled for the interim, replaced with the searing need to capture his phantom. She had been so close. So damned close...

Dario was more animal than human, his instincts more primitive and untamed than any mortal man's came close to being. His former humanity tempered him, made him remember what it was to be vulnerable, but when it came to losing Dawn, the animal in him took over.

Dawn. That which a vampire feared most, that which Dario needed most.

He flew at top speed for over two hours, his eyes scanning the ground, his nostrils seeking a lock on her scent. He was getting nearer. He hadn't quite placed her, but he knew he was closing in.

Chapter Eleven

𝄢

A scraping sound at the window woke her up. Dawn jolted upright in the hotel bed, her breathing labored and eyes wide. Someone — or some*thing* — was outside.

Nervous and shaking, she quietly rose from the bed and made her way toward the window. Heart pounding, she grabbed a fistful of curtain. After saying a quick prayer, she found the courage to thrust the fabric to the side.

Nothing — just a damn bird. She sagged in relief.

Expelling a breath of air, Dawn released the curtain, allowing it to fall back into place. She walked across the room to a nearby sink, splashing her face with cool water. It had been a long twenty-four hours.

Elizabeth. Dario. The near-deaths of the teenage girls. The mad dash to Istanbul, Turkey, on the first flight out of Vienna. She was exhausted.

Why Dawn had come to Istanbul in the first place she didn't know, but she was learning to value her instincts. A scientist always placed importance on gut intuition, but hunting Elizabeth went beyond that. She was attuned to the vampiress somehow, could sense her movements in a way she doubted any others could. They were connected in some morbid, completely indescribable fashion —

The awakened and the awakener.

The sound of the window slowly opening jarred Dawn from her thoughts. She whirled around and struggled for breath, a stiff gust of cold air freezing her, hardening her nipples against the sheer fabric of the T-shirt she'd worn to bed. One second she saw a swirl of smoke, a fog much like that of dry ice, and then a second later…

Him. Dario.

Dawn's eyes rounded as she took a cautious step backward. He was there in her bedroom, larger than life, taller and more formidably muscular than she'd remembered him being. Dressed in his signature head-to-toe black, his hair was as dark as the night, his eyes as blue as sapphires. No fangs, no lit-up green eyes—he looked like a man. A man who radiated a power the likes of which she'd never before known. Her pulse went through the roof.

"I thought vampires couldn't come in unless they were invited," she gasped, backing herself into a wall. "I've read all the books."

His lips sensually curled into a half-smile. "It seems the books were wrong, *bella*."

Dario had never desired a woman with the intensity with which he craved Dawn. She was afraid of him, terrified even, and though he wanted more than anything else to put her fears to rest, the primal part of his brain took over.

He needed to be inside her more than he needed to breathe.

She wore nothing but a nearly see-through white cotton T-shirt and scandalously transparent underwear. Her nipples stabbed against the flimsy garment, arousing him. A triangular, neatly-trimmed thatch of blonde curls was visible from behind the sheer black panties. His cock throbbed, the desire to fuck her, to brand her as his, clouding out everything else from his mind.

There was no hunt for Elizabeth in this moment. There was no stark loneliness. With Dawn standing before him, there was only burning need and a long-sought sense of completion.

"I won't harm you," Dario said thickly, slowly prowling toward her. Her eyes rounded, and a pang of sympathy lanced through him. She feared him, yet he couldn't let her go. "You've my vow."

Her spine straightened, chin thrusting up, despite her tangible panic. He had to admire her strength. "Does a vow mean anything to one like yourself?"

"It means everything, bella."

His sister's nickname had been Bella, the shortened form of Isabella. Under most circumstances, it would have felt strange to call a woman he planned to bed by a name he'd used since childhood in reference to his sibling, but he could think of no other endearment that matched Dawn so perfectly. In his native tongue, *bella* meant beautiful. And that's what she was, inside and out.

There simply was no other word to describe her.

Dario continued his walk toward her, his eyes watching her breasts heave up and down in time with her heavy breathing. She feared him, craved him, loathed and loved him. Confusion ripped through her, tearing her soul apart. He could feel her feelings, sense her every conflicted emotion.

"I've waited a long time to touch you," Dario murmured, his hand finding her chin. "You have no idea just how long."

Her brown gaze collided with his blue one. "What's happening to me?" she asked quietly, her voice catching. "What are you doing to me?"

His mouth covered hers and she whimpered. His hands threaded through her golden hair, possessively clamping onto the soft strands as he kissed her with four hundred years' worth of pent-up passion. His tongue moved with forceful strokes, branding her mouth in the way he meant to brand her body.

Dawn resisted him for a lingering moment, then relented on a small groan, realizing that this was what she wanted too and there was no sense in fighting it any longer. Her arms stole around his middle and she held him, her fingers digging into his back as their kisses turned merciless, almost violent.

Dario guided her toward the bed, never breaking the kiss. Dawn pulled at his shirt, tugging it off and discarding it while they moved as one. Her hands found his trousers next, and he groaned into her mouth when she squeezed his cock before pulling them down.

"It's my turn," Dario growled, tearing his mouth from hers as his hands reached for the sheer cotton shirt, "to undress *you*."

He ripped the shirt from her chest like the animal he was, causing her to show a moment's fear. He was irritated with himself for behaving so boorishly, but couldn't dampen the ravenous need to get inside her as quickly as possible.

Greedy palms cupped her breasts, his thumbs running over her erect nipples. She shivered with arousal and it was all the encouragement he needed. Dario's mouth dove for her chest, his tongue curling around one stiff nipple and drawing it into the warmth of his mouth. Dawn gasped, her head lolling back, her body as limp and compliant as a doll's.

"What are you doing to me?" she whispered again, the question rhetorical this time. "*My God.*"

He nudged her down onto the bed, intimately settling himself between her splayed thighs, then resumed sucking on her nipples. Back and forth, tongue flicking like mad, over and over again.

Dawn writhed and moaned beneath him, her breath expelling on a hiss. The sounds were like an aphrodisiac. Dario needed more, wanted all of her.

He kissed his way down her body, licking her from breasts to belly. He flicked at her navel with his tongue, then went lower still, his mouth kissing her crotch through her panties. She went wild, her hips bucking up.

Dario sucked on her clit through the black silk, her moans and groans making him ache with arousal. His cock was rigid, stiffer than it had ever been before. Needing to taste her, he pulled down her panties and feasted.

Her pussy was warm, tight and delicious. The tangy scent of feminine arousal perfumed the air. Drawing her clit into his mouth, he sucked it hard, wanting to taste her cum.

"Oh God," Dawn gasped, her fingers threading through his hair, pushing his face as close to her cunt as it could go. "Please don't stop!"

He had no intention of it. Not until he got what he wanted.

Her breathing grew increasingly ragged as her thighs trembled around him. Dario sucked harder, vigorously working her clit. She burst on a loud moan, her entire body shaking as her female juices trickled down his throat. He groaned as he drank of her, kissing her sensitive flesh softly while she rode out the wave of ecstasy.

His face surfaced from between her thighs. Dario's nostrils flared as his gaze meandered up her body, from the soft thatch of blonde curls at her mons to the taut belly with a bare hint of fleshiness to her perky breasts with hard, stiff nipples…to her beautiful face bathed in a pool of golden hair.

Bella. There really was no other word to describe her.

As he stared at her, worshipped her with his eyes, a possessiveness that bordered on maniacal lanced through him. She must have sensed the change in him, for her fear became tangible again as he positioned the head of his cock at the entrance of her wet flesh.

"You don't need to fear me," he said gutturally. The tone was perhaps too commanding, but he couldn't help himself. He palmed the base of his penis and prepared to claim what had long been destined to be his. "I need you, Dawn. You have no idea how badly I need you."

Dario stared down into her brown eyes and, on a groan of intense pleasure, sank inside her.

Dawn panted, her fingers digging into the steel of his ass. He wasted no time in claiming her, his swollen cock impaling her cunt, over and over, again and again.

"Dario," Dawn moaned, her tits jiggling with every thrust. It was the first time she'd spoken his name. It only served to get him harder, hotter. "Oh God — *oh yes!*"

He fucked her hard, mercilessly, his animal side taking over. He couldn't stop his eyes from emitting the telltale green, the color they took on whenever he was feeding or overpowered with extreme emotion.

The need to bite her, to drink of her, was overwhelming, but he had made a vow, and he intended to keep it. If he was to taste her blood, there would be no turning back. Next he would feed her *his* blood, and then she would be forced into his world forever...

He wouldn't do that — couldn't do that. It had to be her choice.

Dario slammed in and out of her, every muscle in his body tensed. The sound of flesh slapping against flesh echoed off the walls. The sound and feel of her pussy enveloping him inside, not wanting to let go, made his jaw clench. He fucked her harder and faster, glutting himself on her body.

"Turn over," he growled into her ear, his tone permitting no argument. "Get on all fours."

Dawn did as he'd instructed without question. Putting her weight on her elbows, she arched her back, her round, fleshy ass up in the air. Dario sank into her cunt again, seating himself fully within her, the need to dominate her stealing over him.

She either feigned submission or felt it. Either way, he got what he wanted.

Dario fucked her ruthlessly, mounting her hard, both of them moaning as he pounded her with deep, filling strokes. His strong fingers dug into the flesh of her hips as her tight, wet pussy sucked him back in with every outstroke. He took Dawn harder and faster, deeper and determinedly. Over and over. Again and again. Once, twice, three times more...

He came on a loud, reverberating growl, a sound of dominance and possession. He kept up the frenzied fucking, his cum shooting into her pussy.

Dario took her until exhaustion won out, his strokes coming further and further apart. Unable to do anything but, he heaved out a groan and collapsed on top of her. It was a long while before either of them spoke. Eventually he moved off her, coming down next to her.

"How do you know her?" Dawn finally asked, her back to him. "What did she do to you?"

He didn't pretend not to know which her she was referring to. "Many, many years ago, Elizabeth tortured my sister. She used her like a damned goat, feeding from her and torturing her for weeks. Had I not shown up when I did, she would have killed Isabella."

Silence.

"You must have loved her."

He stared at her back.

"When it comes right down to it, not just any man would sacrifice himself to save someone else. Not even his sister."

Dario stilled. How could Dawn have known that the countess was responsible for making him what he was?

"It was very honorable," she whispered. "She was lucky to have you for a brother."

Her praise was humbling, not to mention undeserved. Perhaps in the world Earth had become throughout the centuries, a brother wouldn't lay down his life for a sister, but such had not been the case four hundred years ago. The family was the center of life, the reason for being.

The very thing Dawn now was to him.

"You are too kind," Dario murmured, his hand reaching out to stroke her back. "Now go to sleep, *bella*."

Chapter Twelve

❧

Several months passed, and Elizabeth continued to elude them. Dario and Dawn had been together all the while, hunting the countess as one. There seemed no end in sight. Like a thought just out of reach, she managed to stay one step ahead.

Oddly and ironically, no dead bodies were being discovered. It was as if Elizabeth had disappeared, or more likely, gone into hiding. Surely the quiet before the storm.

The hunt had taken them all over the world, from the jungles of South America to the mountains of Tibet, to their current location in Bulgaria. She was everywhere, and she was nowhere. Dawn's conscience wanted to find and destroy the countess immediately — her heart didn't mind the delays, accepting that they kept her with Dario.

Dario.

When Elizabeth was dead, she would have no excuse to stay with him. To do so would be cruel, for she realized how intensely he loved her. To watch her grow old and then die without him...

She loved him too much to put him through that.

It was true. She really had grown to love him. He made her feel with a depth she hadn't thought possible in human relationships. Perhaps they *weren't* possible in human relationships. The thought of leaving him, of returning to a world that seemed ordinary and stale without him, was decidedly depressing.

There was only one way to keep Dario by her side, and Dawn knew exactly what it was. But could she do it? Should she do it? She just didn't know.

One night, after they'd finished making love and the sun was threatening to rise, Dario turned to Dawn. Something in his blue eyes gave her pause, and she found that she didn't want him to say whatever it was he was preparing to utter. She placed a gentle finger to his lips.

"Please," Dawn whispered, her heart in her throat, "don't say it."

He closed his eyes briefly, tiredly, and she knew he was going to tell her it was time for her to leave. Withdrawing her finger, he spoke.

"I don't want to lose you, *bella*—"

"Then don't."

"But every night I spend with you makes it more difficult to let you go. If you don't leave me while I sleep this sunrise, I don't know that I can continue to give you a choice in the matter of your mortality."

"Dario..."

"I love you, Dawn," he murmured, a smile enveloping his lips. His eyes traced her face, memorized it. "Forever."

The sun was coming. Dario weakened, his body forcing him to seek sleep whether he wanted it or not.

"And I love you," Dawn whispered to him, watching his eyes slowly close. "Always."

It was a strange reality—loving someone so desperately and genuinely as they loved each other. Every night of the past seven months brought them closer, every day when they rested felt an eternity until they awoke. Dawn had learned to sleep when Dario did, that they could be together during the darkness.

She stared at him long after he fell into his comatose-like sleep, tears welling in her eyes. She hadn't lied. She would love him forever.

Even if fate forced her to leave him.

* * * * *

Dario awoke to an empty hotel room, the only thing left of Dawn her lingering scent. The pain inside was so all-consuming as to be unbearable, yet he knew the question of her future had to be her choice alone. The decision had been made, and he was all alone again.

He wanted to die—the one thing he could not do.

Naked, he stood up on a sigh, then walked to the window and peered out into the black night. Tonight he would need to feed, for his body felt deprived, clamoring for its nourishment.

He could see the animals scurrying below the windowsill, could hear them communicating with one another. The sounds he had grown to find comforting over the centuries held no more allure. Nothing did. She was gone and had taken his heart with her.

"Good evening," a familiar feminine voice cheerfully greeted him, causing Dario to still. He was afraid to turn around and realize he had but imagined her. "I hope you slept well."

He couldn't resist the pull. He turned around slowly, his face haggard and eyes bloodshot.

Dawn frowned. "You look terrible," she chided, giving him a tsk-tsk sound as she plopped her suitcase onto the floor. "I was hoping for a better reception than this."

His eyes searched her face. "I love you, Dawn. You know this. But I—"

She held up a palm. Her expression, once playful, turned serious. "I can't live without you." The palm dropped to her side. "I love you too much to even try."

His heartbeat picked up, his pulse raced.

"I've spent months wrestling with this decision. I didn't think I could go through with it. Hell, I even packed my suitcase and took a taxi to the airport!"

"Why did you come back?" Dario murmured.

Her face gentled. "Because of you," she said softly. "You big dunce."

His lips kicked up into a smile. "Big dunce?"

"Yeah." She grinned. "But a dunce I can't live without."

Dario's smile turned sad. "I want to be with you forever, Dawn, but I don't want you to one day regret the choice, and hate me because of it."

Dawn shook her head. "That would never happen."

"It could."

"It won't."

"How do you know this?"

She sighed, running a hand briskly through her blonde hair. "Remember the conversation you told me you once had with your sister? The one about destinies?"

Dario nodded. All too well.

"Fate brought us together for a reason, Dario. You believe it is your destiny to maintain the balance between good and evil here on Earth, to protect the innocent from the likes of Elizabeth and others of her ilk." Dawn shook her head, her gaze intense. "And I believe it's my destiny to help you."

There went his heart again, beating like an adolescent schoolboy.

"Fate would never ask anyone to take on such a task alone. It's quite obvious I was meant to be with you."

Her persuasive demeanor forced a smile out of him. He could think of nothing he'd ever wanted more than to spend eternity with the woman he loved. "Once I drink of your blood, and you of mine, there is no going back," he warned.

"I know." Dawn rubbed her hands together in anticipation. "I'm pumped for this! I'm ready, Dario. Let's do it."

Her childlike enthusiasm made him grin. "We aren't performing on Broadway to a sold-out crowd, *bella*. We're turning you into a vampiress."

"I know."

Her teeth sank into her lower lip — a habit she'd soon need to rid herself of if she didn't want to pulverize her mouth with her protruding fangs.

"I've only got one question," Dawn asked, looking a little wary.

Dario raised an eyebrow.

"Is this going to hurt?"

"Only a little, my love." He winked. "No more than a pinch."

Her beautiful brown eyes searched his face. "I love you, Dario. I love you so much it hurts."

Indescribable elation tore through him. He drew her into his embrace and she bared her neck to him. "And I love you, Dawn," he promised, his fangs protruding to scrape against her jugular. "But I need to confess something."

"Yes?"

"I lied."

"Huh? Yeeeeeeoch!"

He sucked her delicious blood, the taste headier than anything he could have imagined. When he was finished, he gave her a sheepish look. "You've my apologies, *bella.*"

"You said it wouldn't hurt!" Dawn accused, playfully slapping him on the shoulder. "Just wait until I get my turn!"

Dario threw his head back and laughed. He couldn't wait for it to be her turn.

Her teeth still that of a human's, he made the task easy on her. One vampiric nail jutting out, he made a small incision in his forearm and lifted it to her lips.

Their gazes clashed as she drank. He shuddered, the sensation an erotic one to his kind.

At last the deed was done. She was all his.

They made love that night, clinging to each other later as the sun rose and they both sought the shelter of slumber. A lot of work lay ahead. The search for Elizabeth Bathory wouldn't end until she was captured and destroyed. There would be others like her throughout the years, and Dario would hunt them the same as he hunted the countess. Only now there was a vast difference. He wouldn't have to do it alone.

The years of bitter isolation and loneliness had finally come to an end. Dario had found the light in the dawn—his Dawn.

POLITICALLY INCORRECT:
STALKED

∽

Trademarks Acknowledgement

The author acknowledges the trademarked status and trademark owners of the following wordmarks mentioned in this work of fiction:

Candy Land: Milton Bradley Company Corporation

Chapter One
Somewhere in rural America
Present day

ℭ

She had never been so frightened in her entire life. She knew she was going to die. Her captor would kill her for certain. Or fuck her then kill her. Or torture her, fuck her, then kill her…

Any way you sliced it, she realized she was as good as dead.

Regina Rose shivered from behind the blindfold she wore—the only thing save the gag in her mouth she was presently wearing. Her cornflower blue sundress and modest white cotton panties had been ripped from her body long ago. She wasn't certain at what point her shoes had been snatched from her feet, but in the grand scheme of things, she supposed her shoes shouldn't much matter.

For hours she had been tied up like this—sitting on a chair, her hands cuffed behind her back forcing her breasts forward, the chill in the dank, dark cellar she was being kept in making her nipples stiffen and ache. Her ankles were cuffed too, each one chained to the furthest point on either side of the chair so that her thighs were kept spread wide open, exposing her labia and clit to—

She didn't know. Ice-cold fear trickled down her spine as she wondered for the hundredth time just who this captor was.

He'd said he was a fan. Claimed to be her most devoted fan, in fact.

Oh God, she thought, hysteria rising as her breasts began to heave, *I've been kidnapped by a goddamn psychopath.*

All Regina had ever wanted to do was be a singer. For as long as she could remember, songs had been running through her brain. Hell, she'd written her first song at the age of six. It had been dumb as hell, crooning on and on about lollipops and ice cream, but still it had been a song. "Gumdrop Mountain", she had called it. Her favorite board game, Candy Land, had inspired it.

The older she grew, the more intricate and captivating her songs became. And the more other people—any people—wanted to hear her sing them. She had been a shy, naïve fifteen-year-old when she'd written her first chart-topping song. That one had been about her first infatuation, Adam, and about how Adam had broken her heart when he'd fallen in love with that slutty baby factory Betty Olsen down the road instead of her.

Good ol' Adam Bennett. He might not have given her the time of day, but her first crush had unintentionally made her a rock star. From there Regina had been signed to a major label. A week later she was famous and a millionaire to boot. Betty Olsen, she thought smugly, was still in that two-bit town in Arkansas, probably popping out her twelfth kid from her twelfth common-law husband.

But Regina—well, Regina was living the life of luxury. She was rich and she was famous and she was beautiful and she was...

She stilled, the reality she'd been doing her damnedest to forget slowly returning. She was a naked captive held hostage in the cold cellar of a psychopath, she thought, panic returning with reality. *Oh damn*, she told herself, her nipples growing impossibly stiffer from the numbing chill, *I've got to get loose...*

Desperate and terrified, Regina rattled the handcuffs securing her to the cold metal chair. She opened her mouth to scream, only then remembering she'd been gagged. *Help me!* she wailed mentally. *Somebody please help me!*

The sound of a nearby door creaking open made her still once again. Her heart began slamming in her chest as not one—but two!—bone-chilling sets of footfalls steadily made their way down some steps and toward where she sat. She recalled that her legs were splayed wide apart and thrashed on the chair, hoping to no avail to close them. *This isn't happening,* Regina thought, her large breasts heaving up and down with her labored breathing. *Dear God in heaven, tell me this isn't happening…*

"I don't believe it," a deep, masculine voice murmured. "It's really her."

The second man had an excited grin in his voice. "Regina fuckin' Rose!"

"Holy shit."

"Holy shit is right. Just look at those big titties. And her cunt…"

"She shaves it bald," the first man murmured in a thick voice.

Regina swallowed past the lump of terror in her throat. She simply couldn't believe this was happening. She began to thrash again as the hysteria built, but realized even as she did so she would never get loose. The only thing the thrashing did was make her breasts jiggle up and down. That, in turn, only made her already stiff-with-the-cold nipples ache more. And no doubt gained her captors' undivided attentions.

The overly excitable man, the one with the grin of accomplishment in his voice, she was certain he was the man who had kidnapped her. The same man who had claimed to be her most loyal and devoted fan. The same man who had prattled on at length about how a woman like her probably thought she was too good for him, but he'd show her yet.

She thrashed harder, her heart pounding in her chest, her breasts jiggling like mad, trying in vain to get loose. *Please, God,* she prayed, the hysteria so acute she thought for one brief moment she might have gone insane, *please help me!*

"Don't get yourself all worked up," the first man said in that low whisper of a voice peculiar to him.

She felt a set of large, calloused fingers run over her shaved mons and between her legs. She immediately stilled, her body stiffening, when his thumb found her clit.

"We might let you live," he murmured, his thumb rubbing her clit in slow, methodic circles, "if you give us what we're wanting without a fight."

Regina cried from behind the blindfold, the only sound coming out due to the gag that of a small, guttural groan. She sounded like the chained pet she felt like, she thought hysterically, her entire body shivering. Yesterday she had been happy and content being the famous, beloved Regina Rose. Today she would have given anything to be the slutty, ordinary Betty Olsen.

"Is the camera on?" the first man asked in his low voice.

There was something eerily familiar about that voice, Regina thought. Something causing a spark of déjà vu to knot in her belly.

"It is now," the excited man answered. "Jesus, my dick is hard! Nobody is going to believe this, Adam. Nobody."

Adam, Regina silently gasped. She did know that voice. Her breathing grew impossibly more labored as the reality of the situation struck her:

Adam Bennett. Her first crush. The man who had unwittingly made her a star. He had conspired to kidnap her. And now he was conspiring to rape her...

And quite possibly kill her.

"That's why we've got the camera on, idiot," Adam muttered before swiping his long, warm tongue down her slit. "Mmmm," he murmured as his tongue swirled around her clit and then around her tight hole. "Damn, she tastes as good as I knew she would, Johnny."

Johnny Bennett—Adam's younger brother. Adam's younger, but equally handsome and well-built brother. Both men stood about six feet tall. Both men sported silky jet-black hair and brown eyes. Both men had always worked as bricklayers, their muscles heavy and defined from the strenuous family trade.

Holy. Shit. She was a dead woman.

Regina shivered from behind the gag. She could feel herself growing moist as Adam continued licking up and down her slit and didn't care for the feeling in the slightest. Adam and Johnny Bennett! This just wasn't happening. For years she had wanted Adam — she had prayed to God every night back in Arkansas that one day he would notice her — but sweet Lord above, she had never wanted him like this.

"You asked and you received. Happy birthday, big bro."

Regina's nostrils flared. *Happy birthday?* If she hadn't been gagged her jaw would have dropped open. Her rape and murder was to be a fucking birthday present? She couldn't believe this, simply could not believe it. This had to be a joke. Certainly they would stop before raping her and tell her it was all a joke?

She knew them, for goodness' sake. She could identify them to the authorities. What's more, if they took her like this she most definitely *would* identify them to the authorities. Assuming, she thought, the dumbfounded numbness deserting her in favor of another round of panic, they let her out of this cold, damp cellar alive...

She began to thrash again, the stainless steel handcuffs making loud clanging sounds against the cold metal chair. Her breasts jiggled harder, her labia slammed smack-dab into Adam's awaiting mouth.

Regina mentally screamed again as Johnny's hands came around the back of the chair and cupped her large breasts. She cried from behind the gag when he began massaging her stiff nipples, rolling them around between thumbs and forefingers. *There is no way they will ever let me leave here alive*, she told herself. *No fucking way.*

Rational thought deserted her. Terror reigned supreme. Her heart began slamming so hard in her chest she felt as though she might pass out.

Deep down inside, Regina knew they'd either keep her forever or kill her outright. At the moment she didn't know which scenario to hope for.

Regina Rose. Yesterday's Queen of Pop. Today's Slave of Madness.

Somebody help me!

Chapter Two

∞

Regina groaned from behind the gag as the man she knew in her heart was Adam Bennett slurped her clit into his mouth and sucked it vigorously. "Goddamn," she heard Johnny Bennett mutter from behind her in a thick, aroused voice as he stretched out her nipples, "this bitch has got some fine-ass tits."

Under ordinary circumstances being called a bitch would have caused her to slap a man's face. Under these horrific, terrifying circumstances, all she could do was be grateful they hadn't yet injured her. Johnny tweaked her stiff nipples and pulled them firmly, while Adam sucked hard on her clit. She tried to shake off the arousal the brothers were forcing her body to feel, but couldn't. She'd never had an orgasm before in her life, but her body was feeling so strange that...

Well, she knew something was about to happen. She knew it and she hated them both for making her feel it. *Bastards*, she inwardly seethed, as her belly clenched in a funny way. Somehow, she vowed, somehow she would break free and she would make them both pay for this.

If they didn't kill her first.

Her first captor — Adam — began sucking on her pussy in earnest. She could hear the slurping sounds his mouth was making as his mouth suctioned hard over her hole and clit. Her belly knotted in that funny way again. The feel of her large nipples being tugged at and pulled on made the knot in her stomach coil impossibly tighter.

Oh Lord, Regina thought, her mind in agony. *I'm coming. I know I'm coming.*

She didn't want to have her first orgasm like this, not by force. Her heart rate went over the top. Her breasts heaved like crazy as feelings of frenzy overwhelmed her. She felt like crying, but perversely, the tears simply would not fall. A woman's first orgasm should never be like this. She had dreamed of being loved and cherished, of being wined, dined and romanced...

Regina groaned from behind the gag as the coil in her belly broke loose and she came so hard she felt dizzy. Blood rushed to her face, heating it. Blood rushed to her nipples, making them stab out even further. She wanted to gasp for air, but the gag prevented her from doing so.

Humiliation overwhelmed her senses. She had come for her kidnappers. *Noooo!*

She heard Johnny make an appreciative sound in the back of his throat before latching his mouth around one of her aching, swollen nipples and sucking on it. "Mmmm," Adam murmured as he lapped up the juice her pussy had made from its tight, tiny hole. "You taste as good as I knew you would," he rasped as if to himself.

This isn't happening, Regina mentally wailed for what felt the thousandth time. *This is not fucking happening! You're supposed to be my hero, Adam! You're supposed to be my hero, not the villain!*

She wanted to scream. She needed to scream. Her breathing was labored. Her mind was splintered. She felt as though she might pass out from the adrenaline overflow her body continually bombarded her with. She just needed to *fucking scream.*

The handcuffs securing her ankles to the chair were removed. The handcuffs securing her hands to the chair were unclasped long enough to refasten them together above her head. Finally—finally!—the gag was ripped from her mouth. Regina opened her mouth and screamed long and loud as the brothers pulled her up from the chair and dragged her down onto the cold earthen ground, her slight naked body between their two huge, muscular ones.

"Help me!" Regina wailed, the shrieking sound high-pitched enough to curdle milk. "Somebody help me! Somebody please — "

A stinging backhand across the face made her see stars. The pain was jarring, numbing, made her feel momentarily disoriented. *Oh God, this wasn't happening.*

"Stop it," Adam hissed from above her. "I'll gag you again if you make another sound."

No, Adam, no! Regina thought in cold, icy panic. *You cannot be like this. You were always my hero. God fucking damn you!*

Johnny secured the handcuffs that held her hands together above her head to a large iron spike jutting out of the ground. At least she was pretty sure it was Johnny. She was still blindfolded so it was difficult to judge who was doing what. All Regina knew was she wanted the nightmare to end.

"Please don't hurt me," Regina begged, half crying and half whimpering. She felt ready to lose her mind. "I'll do anything you say," she gasped between quiet sobs, "if you promise not to kill me."

Silence. Long and frightening.

Finally, at long last, the blindfold was slowly removed. Regina squinted, her terrified blue eyes straining to readjust from total blackness to what felt like painfully intense light. It took her eyes a long moment to focus, but when they did she found herself gasping.

She had known in her heart Adam and Johnny Bennett were her kidnappers. She just hadn't wanted to believe it, still didn't want to believe it. But there was no sense in denying it any longer. Her heart rate went into overdrive when her wild-eyed gaze clashed first with Johnny's...and then with Adam's.

She swallowed hard, the knot in her throat feeling tight and watermelon big. "Please," Regina pleaded, her large breasts heaving with her labored breathing, "please don't do this."

She saw a flicker of something—guilt perhaps?— permeate Adam's features for a fraction of a second. But then he schooled them into the mask of steel he'd worn since she'd been a kid and clenched his jaw unforgivingly.

Why did it have to be like this? Regina thought with as much grief as hysteria. *Why? Why? Why?* She had loved Adam when she was fifteen—and if she were honest, long before that. She would have given anything to be with him. But she didn't want him like this—never like this.

And oh, he was as handsome as ever. Perhaps even more so than what he'd once been. In the few years it had been since last she'd seen him, his bricklayer's body had gotten impossibly more cut with muscular definition. He was more tan. His hair even seemed darker than the shiny inky black it had always been. He'd developed a couple of grim laugh lines around the eyes, but otherwise he hadn't aged much in the past three years.

"You got away from me once," Adam murmured in a thick voice, his heavy-lidded brown gaze raking over her naked body. "It won't happen twice."

Chapter Three

ဢ

Regina Rose was an eighteen-year-old virgin who'd been famous since the age of fifteen. She hadn't had time in those three short years to date much, let alone get in a relationship serious enough to warrant giving her virginity up.

A surge of power combined with lust overtook Adam as he sat back and simply stared at the gorgeous, naked, helpless woman splayed out before him. *Regina Rose*, he thought, his jaw clenching. He'd wanted her since she was fifteen. She'd been too young back then to do the things he'd wanted to do to her—like pop that sweet little cherry—but she was old enough to take him now. She was only eighteen to his thirty-five, but eighteen was very legal. Of course, stealing Regina's sweet little cherry wasn't exactly legal, but he'd wanted it for so long that he no longer cared.

And oh yes, he thought, as he buried his stubbled face between her legs once again and his tongue found her tight little hole, his Regina was still as pure as the driven snow. An egotistical rock star she might be now, but she was still tight, hot and completely untried. He couldn't wait to change that. His body tensed and his cock dripped pre-cum at the very thought.

Adam had always been the type of man to go after what he wanted until he got it. He never thought he'd go so far as to resort to kidnapping and rape to accomplish a goal, but then there was nothing he wouldn't have done to possess Regina. No matter what happened after it was over, he knew it would be worth it. He'd be looking into her eyes as he thrust deep inside her juicy cunt and popped her cherry. Anything was worth that.

He saw his younger brother stand up to undress, his cock that was almost as big as Adam's springing free. Truth be told, Adam didn't like to share—especially not Regina—but a deal was a deal and he'd see his end of the bargain through. Johnny would get to have his fun too for helping to kidnap the princess from her secluded palace. When it was over his brother would never touch Regina again, but tonight the rules would be a bit different.

Adam realized he was a possessive, dominating man. He was more jealous than he didn't know what and hated sharing anything, let alone the eighteen-year-old virgin lying spread-eagle before him. But for tonight and only tonight he would have to let that jealousy go. It wouldn't be easy, but he could do it.

Besides, he reminded himself as he drew Regina's tiny, swollen clit into the warmth of his mouth and sucked on it, it was worth it. Johnny had helped him steal away the sweet little pussy he'd dreamt of owning for three solid years. He thrust his tongue into her tight, hot, virgin cunt and damn near passed out from the excitement. He could feel her cherry there and wanted it bad.

Adam was the type who took what he wanted, but he could hardly be called stupid. The worry that the police might find Regina was in the back of his mind, keeping his senses extra alert and vigilant, but no way would they find her before he sank his cock nine inches deep into her tight, sexy pussy. By then Adam would have had his one wish come true so nothing else mattered. Not prison, not anything.

Adam's nostrils flared as he breathed in the scent of her arousal. She probably thought she was too good for him now. Her rock star to his blue-collared laborer. But at this moment in time the Arkansas bricklayer wielded total and complete power over the transplanted L.A. singer—the very situation he'd masturbated to while fantasizing over for the past three years.

Regina Rose and her cherry were the best birthday presents a man could ever ask for. He intended on savoring both.

Regina's terrified blue eyes widened when she saw Johnny Bennett grab his thick cock by the base and walk toward her. His brown eyes so much like his brother's were heavy-lidded with arousal. His well-cut, muscled body that was all but identical to Adam's looked corded and tense, as though he couldn't wait to sink his cock into her.

Oh no, Regina thought, her breathing growing labored again. *Here it comes. I saved my virginity for a special man and now I'll be losing it to two rapists.*

"Please," Regina pleaded in vain, "please don't do this." She forced a shaky smile to her lips. Her breathing was so heavy she felt as though she might faint. "I promise I won't tell anyone if you let me go. I promise!"

"Shhh," Johnny whispered as he came down to his knees beside her face. "Open your mouth like a good girl and don't speak." His jaw clenched. "If you don't cooperate, you'll be gagged again. Only next time I'll make sure it hurts." He ran his long, calloused fingers through her silky, waist-length blonde hair, fanning it out behind her head. The gesture was almost reverent and at complete odds with his otherwise frightening behavior.

Terrified, panicked and not knowing what else to do, Regina opened her mouth like a baby bird waiting to be fed. Her heart slammed inside her chest as Johnny poked at the entrance to her mouth with his cock. A wet, salty taste assaulted her taste buds. Was that what male ejaculate tasted like? *Why do I have to find out like this?*

"Open wide," Johnny murmured, his voice thick. "Take all of me in, baby."

She opened wider. Cold, unadulterated fear lanced through her. Her breasts began to heave again, causing Adam to palm one. He massaged one of her stiff nipples with his left hand while his right hand continued to play with her clit. She hated him for making her feel arousal while Johnny was forcing his cock between her lips, but there it was.

Johnny groaned as he sank his rock-hard manhood all the way into her mouth, his left knee now next to her face while his right leg bent up, giving him room to move back and forth from the side of her. Regina instinctively choked, having never had a cock in her mouth before, let alone in her throat. She must have unthinkingly clamped down a little bit, because he hissed and grabbed her roughly by the hair.

"If you hurt me, I hurt you," Johnny growled. "Now relax and take my cock all the way."

He meant what he'd said, Regina knew. She supposed she should have felt hysterical, but oddly enough, giving her a task to concentrate on somehow made her heart rate come down a little. Not much, but a little. She opened her full lips up wide, accepting Johnny's next stroke without choking this time. He hissed with delight in the back of his throat.

"That's a good little girl," he rasped, his stomach muscles tensing as he slowly sank his cock in and out of her mouth. He held her head in place with his hands and slowly rotated his hips to continuously feed her cock. "Mmm, you feel good. So damn good." His voice sounded like rapture, nirvana. "Now moan for me so I know you like it."

Regina stilled. Her blue eyes widened. He wanted her to moan, pretending she liked it? Sweet Lord, she refused to do that. If the brothers were going to rape her, she'd be damned if she'd pretend to want it.

The pressure Adam had been applying to her clit and nipple intensified. She moaned from around Johnny's cock. Johnny sank it in deeply, his breath catching as he began to fuck her face in faster strokes.

"Shit, yeah," Johnny growled, his hips pistoning back and forth from where he sat above her. He fucked her face harder, his breathing growing increasingly labored with every plunge he made into her mouth and throat.

Adam buried his face between Regina's legs once again. He sucked on her clit vigorously, making her moan loudly from around Johnny's cock. Johnny pumped her face faster, every muscle in his body coiling as he prepared to come.

"Drink me, baby," Johnny growled as he sank his cock between her lips. "Drink me all up."

He came on a groan, the masculine sound reverberating throughout the dimly lit, isolated cellar. Regina's eyes widened from around his cock as it jerked in her mouth and shot out a load of warm, salty cum. It was a straight shot down her throat, so she swallowed most of it without tasting.

"Lick it all up," Johnny murmured as Adam's clit sucking intensified. The coil in her belly tightened again. "Clean out the little hole."

She did as she'd been instructed, sucking vigorously at the tiny hole in the head of his cock while the coil in her belly broke loose. Regina moaned from around Johnny's cock as she came, extracting all of his juice like a baby nursing a bottle.

"That's a good girl," Johnny panted as he plucked his cock from between her full lips with a popping sound. He moved to the right of her and collapsed, his mouth finding one of her tits and latching on to the nipple there.

Her overwhelmed, skittish gaze found Adam's. He looked angry, she thought, her heartbeat going back into overdrive. She could tell he hadn't liked watching his brother fuck her mouth. So why had he let him do it?

Regina watched in fear as Adam stood up and undressed. His chest was wide and chiseled, a sprinkling of black hair covering it and tapering down into a thin line below his navel before disappearing into his faded blue jeans. Her breathing grew labored as his jeans were thrust down next, revealing a cock that was even longer and thicker than Johnny's. It stabbed up from a nest of curly black hair, looking big, frightening and very eager.

Sweet Lord, Regina thought, her eyes bulging from rekindled hysteria. She doubted she could handle something that big between her thighs. She implicitly understood Adam planned to steal her virginity, but for the life of her she couldn't figure out how he would stuff that huge thing into her tight, untried hole without killing her.

"Please," Regina pleaded once more, desperation tinting her voice. "I've never been with a man before! Adam, please don't do this. Please!"

He stilled. Intense brown eyes met frightened blue ones.

"I've been planning this moment for three years, Regina Rose," Adam murmured. "You best lay back and enjoy it."

Chapter Four

ஐ

Adam saw Regina's breathing grow shaky and sporadic as he settled himself between her thighs. Johnny's head was buried between her breasts, his mouth continually latching on to one plump nipple and sucking on it before going back to the other one and doing the same.

He supposed he should have felt guilty for taking her virginity like this, and maybe he did just a little bit. The guilt, however, could not compete with the rush of lust and power surging through his blood. He wanted Regina's cherry more than he wanted to breathe. He was about thirty seconds away from having it.

Damn if his heart didn't turn over just looking at her wide frightened blue eyes and voluptuous, helpless body. Her sexy blonde hair fanned out behind her in the way he'd often envisioned seeing it. The scent of her last orgasm still permeated his nostrils, making him breathe in deeply as he guided his long, thick cock to the opening of her tiny shaved cunt. She tensed up when he nestled the head against her teeny little hole, her breathing heavy with fear of the unknown.

Goddamn, he was already wanting to come.

"P-please, Adam," Regina whispered, her voice trembling. "Please don't do this. I w-wanted my first time to be special."

His nostrils flared at the sound of his own name. With jealousy. With possessiveness. With determination.

"This is special," Adam said thickly, his cock poised at her tight pussy hole. His jaw steeled. "I'm taking what should have been mine long ago."

Teeth gritting, his gaze clashed with hers. Beads of perspiration broke out on his forehead. On a groan he sank into her cunt, seating himself to the hilt.

"Shit," Adam rasped, ignoring her cry of pain. Oh Christ, he'd never felt anything so tight and hot and sticky. He moaned when he felt her hymen give way, the feeling of power gave him beyond anything he'd ever felt before. "Goddamn, your cunt feels good, baby," he said thickly.

Regina gasped, a tear trickling down her cheek. "It hurts," she said in a voice that sounded like a little girl's.

He'd popped her cherry. Christ—he'd actually popped *the* Regina Rose's little cherry. The need to come was urgent, but he forced it away. He wanted to savor this moment, to fuck her cunt a long, gluttonous time.

Adam bent his neck and licked the tear away. That accomplished, he grabbed her by the hips and came up to his knees. He rolled his hips slowly, his dark eyes narrowing in lust as he watched his big, hard cock sink into her hot, juicy pussy. It was the most arousing sight on God's green earth.

"It'll start feeling good," he rasped. "Just lay back and enjoy it, baby."

Johnny's tongue coiled around one of Regina's nipples like a snake. She moaned just a little bit, relaxing more and more. Adam's teeth gritted at the exquisitely tight feel of her small, barely broken-in cunt. Shit, it was so tight. He wanted this moment to last forever.

"How's it feeling?" Adam asked in a low, aroused voice as he slowly sank in and out of her hot pussy. He could hear her cunt suctioning him back in, making him impossibly harder. "Does my baby girl like being fucked with a big dick now?"

She was given no time to answer. Johnny, who'd been jerking his cock hard as he watched Adam fuck her, came up to his knees and shoved his cock back into Regina's awaiting mouth. She closed her eyes and sucked on it, moaning every time Adam sank into her again.

Oh yes, she liked it. Regina Rose was his hot little slut. From virgin to fuck-toy in the blink of an eye.

Adam's fingers sank into the flesh of her hips as he picked up the pace of their fucking. He sank it into her fully on a groan, taking her faster and deeper, harder and branding.

Christ, he thought, his jaw clenching hotly, he was going to spurt soon. He didn't want to spurt. He felt like a virgin himself, like a boy sinking into his first pussy. Like he wanted to claim it all night long, sucking it and fucking it, and doing whatever he wanted to do to it. Of course, he reminded himself, he *could* do those things all night long. Maybe longer than that. He had covered Johnny's tracks well. It would take the cops a while to find Regina, star or no star.

Regina groaned from around Johnny's cock, her huge tits jiggling with each of Adam's penetrating thrusts. His nostrils flared as he fucked her, his cock pounding in and out of her with barely controlled violence.

"You're so tight, baby," Adam ground out, his face squinting as if in pain. He clutched her hips more roughly and banged her cunt like crazy. "I'm coming in my gorgeous slut's pussy," he growled, sinking his cock into her tight, juicy hole over and over, again and again.

The brothers groaned at the same time, one of them spurting hot seed into Regina's cunt while the other one shot a load into her mouth. She drank Johnny up while Adam continued to fuck her, a loud groan ripping from the depths of his throat as her pussy milked his cock of seed.

A few seconds later, Johnny rolled away and Adam collapsed on top of Regina, barely able to breathe, let alone stand. He buried his face between her huge breasts and sucked on each nipple like a poor kid with no candy money who'd found two lollipops. Shit. He was more content than he'd ever thought possible.

It had all been worth it, Adam realized. The years of planning. The months of stalking. The agony every time he saw her out, dating some little pansy guy. The worry over whether or not he'd get arrested before his plan was executed.

None of it mattered anymore. Not a bit. Because Regina Rose's sweet little cherry belonged irrevocably to Adam Bennett.

Chapter Five

ഇ

The brothers fucked Regina twice more before taking their leave of her. First, Adam fucked her cunt while Johnny watched and tweaked her nipples, then they switched places, blindfolded her, and Johnny fucked her pussy while Adam played with her tits. After that last sex session they left, stalking off to only who knows where.

They left her naked, blindfolded, and gagged down in the chilly cellar for what felt like hours. She was still on the ground, her cuffed hands secured to an iron post above her head. A couple of critters scampered by now and again, scaring her something awful...

Scaring her to the point that Regina was actually hoping the brothers would come back.

She hated admitting it to herself—she really did—but once Adam had sunk in all the way and something inside her had torn, the sex had actually started feeling pretty good. After that she'd been able to take their huge cocks without too much trouble. She was a little bit sore, but nothing unmanageable.

She would have to keep reminding herself of that. Maybe if she was good and did her best to please the brothers, she desperately told herself, maybe they would let her live. Perhaps they'd even let her leave...one day.

There were so many things Regina still wanted out of life. Her singing aspirations had been realized, that much was true, but what about falling in love and getting married? What about bearing her husband's children and family barbecues on the Fourth of July? She sighed. It just couldn't end like this. All Regina had ever really wanted was to be loved. She had fooled herself into thinking fame could replace that. There was no substitute for the real thing.

It was probably another hour before the sound of footfalls again made their way into the creepy cellar. By the time the brothers returned, Regina had talked herself into doing whatever they wanted, saying whatever they wanted, and thinking whatever they wanted—all with a smile of welcome on her face.

She would get through this ordeal yet, she adamantly reminded herself. She would be set free one day and life would return to normal. Something inside told her nothing would ever be the same again, but she refused to listen to that voice right now. As soon as the gag was removed from her mouth, she smiled, spread her legs wide, and asked to be fucked again.

"Please," Regina breathed, "I'd give anything to feel your big cock inside me again, Adam." She could feel him still, though she couldn't see him.

"Is that a fact?" he purred, coming down on top of her and burying his face between her big breasts. He seemed to love sucking on her nipples, nipples that were kept stiff by the merciless chill of the cellar.

"Yes," she whispered. She reared her hips up to tempt him with her pussy. She wanted to make him happy. If he was happy, maybe he'd let her leave this awful, frightening place. "Maybe Johnny will want to fuck me again too."

The blindfold was ripped from her eyes. She blinked, her gaze adjusting then finally focusing on the pissed-off male lying between her spread thighs. Adam had never looked more possessive of her than he looked in this moment. She found herself feeling more frightened than ever before.

"There will be no more Johnny," Adam ground out, his nostrils flaring. Reaching up over her head, he unhooked the handcuffs from the pole in the ground before releasing them from her wrists. That accomplished, he grabbed Regina by the back of the head and stared broodingly down into her face. "I've seen to that. Now turn over, get up on all fours, and offer me my cunt."

Her blue eyes went wide, wondering as she was what Adam had meant by declaring he'd "seen to" Johnny. Sweet Lord above, if he'd do away with his own brother she was as good as dead! Her breasts began heaving in time with her labored breathing, but she did as she was told and rolled over onto her belly.

"Offer me my hot slut's tight cunt," Adam ordered. "*Now.*"

Regina immediately went on all fours, ass up, face down. She used her newly freed hands to spread apart her clean-shaven pussy lips. "Please fuck your hot slut's tight cunt," she whispered in a small little voice. She wiggled her ass for effect.

It didn't take Adam but a moment to get into the spirit of things. With a growl, he sank into his prisoner, making her gasp. He grabbed her big tits and held on as he started to ride her, moaning as he plunged his cock into her tight pussy over and over again.

"My cunt feels hot and sweet, baby," Adam gritted between thrusts. "Throw that pussy back at me."

Regina immediately obeyed, her hips slamming back as hard as they could, meeting him thrust for thrust. Catering to the bricklayer's every whim was a far cry from the pampered, spoiled life of stardom she was used to living, but all thoughts of that life now seemed distant, almost as though they'd never been.

She moaned long and loud as he fucked her, her tits jiggling in his palms with every thrust. "Fuck me harder," she begged, throwing her hips back at him. "*Please fuck me harder.*"

He gave her what she wanted, banging her like the obsessed lover he was until that coil in her belly she now recognized as the building climax sprang loose and she groaned as a powerful orgasm ripped through her belly.

"Goddamn, my little slut is one hot bitch," Adam gritted out, pulling his cock from her tight, juicy cunt. He poised the head of his cock at her other virgin hole before smacking her on the ass until she yelped. "Now I want to know how your ass feels, baby," he groaned out as he slid the head in. Regina gasped. "Tell me how much you like my big dick in your little tiny asshole."

Adam sank his huge cock all the way into her ass, causing Regina to moan loudly. Now she'd been taken in every way there was for a man to take a woman. There was nothing virgin about Regina Rose any longer.

She threw her hips back at him, making him growl as he fucked her. "I love your cock in my ass," Regina moaned. "Fuck me harder, Adam. Please fuck me harder!"

She felt his body tense up, heard his breathing hitch, and knew he was about to come. She threw a coy smile over her shoulder as she watched his intense face scrunch up and his orgasm break loose. Adam's masculine bellow of satisfaction could probably be heard a mile off, she thought, no longer wanting the police to find her.

Regina Rose was Adam Bennett's hot little slut. She loved it.

Epilogue

ഇ

"I think," Adam growled as he stood up and held out his hand to Regina, "that a woman who'd never had a cock up her ass before would have cried a little or something."

Regina grinned, then stuck her tongue out at her husband. Okay, so she wasn't eighteen, she was forty. And so she wasn't a rock star, she was a schoolteacher. But who knew what could have happened if she'd run off to L.A. all those years back instead of marrying the handsome, loving bricklayer standing before her. And for that matter, who cared, either.

Regina Rose Bennett didn't care. All she had ever wanted in life was Adam Bennett. He was her every fantasy, her every dream, and thank God, her daily reality for the past twenty years. Her smile turned soft.

"Thanks for a," she cleared her throat, "memorable fortieth birthday present. I've been having that *eighteen-year-old-virgin-is-kidnapped-and-forced-to-submit-to-two-fine-as-all-hell-alpha-men* fantasy since my early twenties."

Adam grunted. "You're welcome," he muttered into her hair as he pulled her close and hugged her tightly. "You fulfilled my *two-women-at-once* fantasy with yourself and that prostitute last year in Amsterdam on *my* fortieth birthday. Now you've had yours fulfilled with a male prostitute in Paris and me. I'd say we're done with the fantasies now," he growled in the possessive broach-no-argument voice she had always found so comforting.

Regina's head came up. She frowned, though her eyes danced with amusement. "I really had to work hard to make myself believe that prostitute with his French accent was your brother, though. I asked for tall, dark and handsome. You brought me short, blond and questionably good-looking. Sweet Lord, Adam, I about had heart failure when you ripped the blindfold off and I saw Toulouse Lautrec ready to mount me. I'm probably half a foot taller!"

Another grunt. And a small smile. "And in Amsterdam I asked for a redhead built like a brick shithouse. You brought me Medusa's twin sister." He frowned. "The only similarity she had to a brick shithouse was the way she smelled after she accidentally passed gas when she bent over to put her clothes back on."

Regina had to grin at that. At least her guy had been decent-looking enough. "Yeah, well, there is that." Her blonde eyebrows slowly drew together.

"What?" Adam asked a bit warily. He nervously avoided her gaze.

Regina's eyes narrowed. "The blindfold…" She frowned. "That was *you* fucking me, wasn't it? You didn't let Shorty screw me?"

Adam's nostrils flared. "Hell no, I didn't," he growled. "You sucking him off was more than enough." His hand slashed definitively through the air. "I tried, Regina, I really did, but I couldn't see it through, okay?"

She pretended to pout. It lasted maybe a second before her face broke into a grin. "That's okay. Remember when you were blindfolded and Medusa's twin sister was riding you?"

Adam's face broke into a sly smile. "That was you, baby?" he murmured.

"Uh-huh."

"Brat."

She laughed as she reached for her cotton sundress and pulled it back on. "I guess we're two of a kind," she said as she stepped into her leather sandals.

"We always have been," Adam replied, his tone growing serious. He drew his wife back into his arms and stared down into her eyes. "I love you, Regina Rose. Not a day goes by I don't thank God I have you and the kids."

Regina's gaze was warm and welcoming—just like always. "Me too. I love you so much, Adam." She took a deep breath and smiled. "Come on, honey. Let's go home."

He winked. "Vive la Arkansas."

Why an electronic book?

We live in the Information Age — an exciting time in the history of human civilization, in which technology rules supreme and continues to progress in leaps and bounds every minute of every day. For a multitude of reasons, more and more avid literary fans are opting to purchase e-books instead of paper books. The question from those not yet initiated into the world of electronic reading is simply: *Why?*

1. *Price.* An electronic title at Ellora's Cave Publishing and Cerridwen Press runs anywhere from 40% to 75% less than the cover price of the exact same title in paperback format. Why? Basic mathematics and cost. It is less expensive to publish an e-book (no paper and printing, no warehousing and shipping) than it is to publish a paperback, so the savings are passed along to the consumer.

2. *Space.* Running out of room in your house for your books? That is one worry you will never have with electronic books. For a low one-time cost, you can purchase a handheld device specifically designed for e-reading. Many e-readers have large, convenient screens for viewing. Better yet, hundreds of titles can be stored within your new library — on a single microchip. There are a variety of e-readers from different manufacturers. You can also read e-books on your PC or laptop computer. (Please note that Ellora's Cave does not endorse any specific brands.

You can check our websites at www.ellorascave.com or www.cerridwenpress.com for information we make available to new consumers.)

3. *Mobility.* Because your new e-library consists of only a microchip within a small, easily transportable e-reader, your entire cache of books can be taken with you wherever you go.

4. *Personal Viewing Preferences.* Are the words you are currently reading too small? Too large? Too... ANNOYING? Paperback books cannot be modified according to personal preferences, but e-books can.

5. *Instant Gratification.* Is it the middle of the night and all the bookstores near you are closed? Are you tired of waiting days, sometimes weeks, for bookstores to ship the novels you bought? Ellora's Cave Publishing sells instantaneous downloads twenty-four hours a day, seven days a week, every day of the year. Our webstore is never closed. Our e-book delivery system is 100% automated, meaning your order is filled as soon as you pay for it.

Those are a few of the top reasons why electronic books are replacing paperbacks for many avid readers.

As always, Ellora's Cave and Cerridwen Press welcome your questions and comments. We invite you to email us at Comments@ellorascave.com or write to us directly at Ellora's Cave Publishing Inc., 1056 Home Avenue, Akron, OH 44310-3502.

THE
⚷ ELLORA'S CAVE ⚷
LIBRARY

Stay up to date with Ellora's Cave Titles in
Print with our Quarterly Catalog.

TO RECIEVE A CATALOG,
SEND AN EMAIL WITH YOUR NAME
AND MAILING ADDRESS TO:

CATALOG@ELLORASCAVE.COM

OR SEND A LETTER OR POSTCARD
WITH YOUR MAILING ADDRESS TO:

CATALOG REQUEST
C/O ELLORA'S CAVE PUBLISHING, INC.
1056 HOME AVENUE
AKRON, OHIO 44310-3502

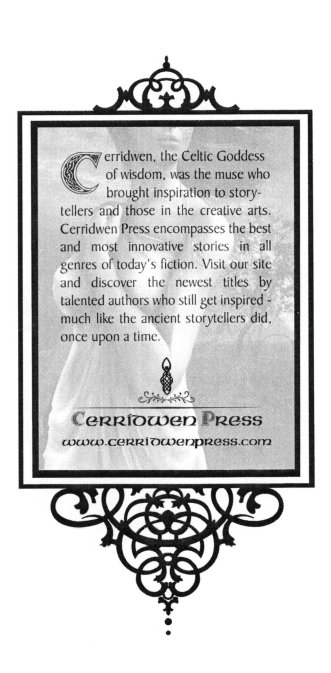

erridwen, the Celtic Goddess of wisdom, was the muse who brought inspiration to storytellers and those in the creative arts. Cerridwen Press encompasses the best and most innovative stories in all genres of today's fiction. Visit our site and discover the newest titles by talented authors who still get inspired - much like the ancient storytellers did, once upon a time.

Cerridwen Press

www.cerridwenpress.com